PANDEMIC PURSUIT

DEV ARVIND CHATURVEDI

INDIA • SINGAPORE • MALAYSIA

ISBN
Paperback 979-8-89544-548-8
Hardcase 979-8-89632-431-7

Contents

Prologue

THE BEGINNING

Wuhan, November 2019

Wuhan Institute of Virology is a maze of silver-gray structures located on the outskirts of the city of Wuhan. Behind these monochrome metallic exteriors are the countless research and testing labs holding secrets that could potentially endanger mankind. What further reinforces the solemn atmosphere are the security personnel, clad in black from head to toe, forming a steady perimeter throughout the premises.

The compound is sparsely softened by scattered patches of green-a few trees and shrubs, offering a rare touch of life in this lifeless premises. The institute is locked down like a bank vault. Its Level V security status commands three layered security. High above, armed drones carry out surveillance, electrified fences enclose the perimeter, while underground sensors detect the slightest movement or intrusion.

A single gateway serves as both point of entry and exit to the institute which is guarded by the elite police force along with the Belgian Malinois dogs. Not even the Director and VIP visitors are afforded personal transport within these walls. All who enter and exit must pass through an X-ray chamber to ensure that nothing slips in or out from this compound.

Inside the labs, utmost care is taken to ensure that various viruses under development do not infect the staff. Nobody is permitted to handle the development process physically with their own hands. It is all remote controlled, like the doctors performing a keyhole surgery.

So, how did the infected bat find its way from the lab to the Wuhan wild animals' market? Or was it the vial of the Corona virus that was taken out and dropped in the central market of Wuhan? How did it happen?

Scientists from thirty-two countries are working at the WVI, including Americans, Japanese, Russians, Italians, British, and North and South Koreans. Scientists of Indian origin aren't allowed to work here.

On 15th November 2019, a power malfunction occurred at the WVI at around 6 p.m. when the majority of the scientists were exiting the institute. All of them were subjected to a full body search in the absence of the x-ray machine.

The first person, as reported by South Morning China Post to have contacted the virus, was a 55-year-old man from Hubei province, who tested positive on 17th November 2019 and reportedly had no link with the wet/seafood market. Wuhan is the capital of Hubei province.

Was the virus transmitted by a bat to a human through another animal, possibly a pangolin? Or was it a deliberately planned and executed biological strike?

GAME ZERO

San Siro Stadium, Milan, Italy

More than 40,000 fans gathered on the night of February 19, 2020, at the iconic San Siro Stadium in Milan, Italy, to watch the Champions League game between Atlanta and Valencia. The stadium was filled to capacity with supporters of both teams. The majority of them were Italians, but there were also fans from across the world, including Spain, Russia, and China. Atlanta was a team new to the Champions League but was riding a crest of success, while Valencia, an old warhorse, was going through a patchy phase. Both teams dearly wanted to win and were locked in a see-saw battle.

In the crowd, there were a few East Asians huddled together, cheering for Atlanta. One of them was wearing a trench coat with big pockets. At half-time, he took out a cigar case from his pocket, opened it, and took out a Havana cigar. The Group of East Asians got up in sync and moved towards the restrooms. In the crowd, Mr. Trench coat missed a step, and the cigar slipped out of his hand. Without pausing to retrieve his cigar, he moved out with his group while the other spectators were rushing back to their seats. The group of East Asians did not return to watch the balance of the game.

While Atlanta won the game 4-1, its goalkeeper, Marco Sportiello, tested positive for the Coronavirus, as did one-third of Valencia's squad. As far as the fans were concerned, it could not be ascertained how many of the 40,000-plus fans were affected by the virus. Italy remained the European nation with the most number of infected cases, and Spain was a close second.

Chapter 1

Sambar Soldier Scholar Spy

My name is Vidya Sagar Aiyar. I work for WAP, a software giant whose origins are in the USA. Its sprawling offices straddle the globe today; the company joke is that the sun now does not set on the WAP empire. However, the Coronavirus pandemic has hit WAP, as it has the rest of the world, and the WAP senior management sought me out, and three others to develop an application to overcome the virus. WAP believes, as does the rest of the world that a suitable mobile application can overcome Coronavirus. Why was I chosen from the thousands of WAP employees? In fact, they sought my advice on it, as they have been doing on many complex issues earlier. Although it may sound boastful, they've asked me to head the Coronavirus Killer Application Task Force.

So why me? The answer lies in my surname, which influenced their choice. My last name, Aiyar, by default, designates me as a Tamil Brahmin (Tambram), a group often regarded as an 'Ocean of Knowledge.' We are thought to be naturally intelligent, seekers of knowledge, vegetarians, and steadfast in our convictions. Tambrams are tradition-bound, haughty, and opinionated.

Some say that we have used our superior intellect to exploit others. In the 1950s, big anti-Tambram protests rocked my native state of Tamil Nadu, which forced many of us to leave our homes in search of higher education, jobs, and business. Tamil Nadu's loss was the world's gain. Sundar Pichai, Raghuram Rajan, Indira Nooyi, N. Chandrasekaran, N. Srinivasan, Viswanathan Anand, Subramanian Swamy, General Padmanabhan, and T.N. Seshan—this list of Tambrams goes on, as they continue to shape the global landscape. We are a small community, but our gene pool is unique and has endowed us with strong academic qualities.

You will find us in Silicon Valley with leading business houses, at NASA, ISRO, and ISS, as super-speciality doctors, in the civil services, and, of course, in cinema. Don't believe me? Just Google Hema Malini, the Dream Girl; look up Jayalalitha or Vijayantimala. You could also search for Tambram actresses in Bollywood, and I assure you, your jaw will drop.

You may find the name of General Padmanabhan a bit out of place in those listed above because we are basically not a warrior caste revelling in blood and gore, but scholars who find the pen mightier than the sword. So, General Paddy is a bit of an outlier, but he is a distant relative of mine and an intellectual to boot. I met him when I was in my final school year, and he was posted in Delhi as the Chief of Army Staff; my parents took me to his residence: Army House. He had just returned from India Gate after attending a Guard of Honour and was dressed in full regalia. I was quite taken in by his persona, and he then literally bowled me over with his oratory skills. I decided then to follow his footsteps and join the Indian Army. So, while in my final year at school, I took the National Defence Academy competitive exam, and lo and behold, I stood second on the merit list; I am not boasting, but I had hardly spent time preparing for the academically challenging exam taken by over 300,000 aspirants from across the country. I joined NDA at the age of seventeen and very soon realised that my cup of coffee was different. A genetically empowered being was expected to bathe in common open showers, undergo incessant physical toughening and instil obedience to orders through endless hours of senseless drills by robot-like drill ustaads, instructors, for whom disciplined routine was a religion. I was down for the count very early on. Like a zombie, one went through the academic classes, often sleeping with eyes open; yes, it is doable!

Throughout the term, written tests were periodically held, and I aced almost all of them. The term end results showed my CGPA at 8.3 out of a possible 9, an all-time record in the Academy. Fortunately, the Commandant, Air Marshal Bottlewala, a smart, flamboyant fighter pilot, spotted me while I was treading back all alone after three hours of equestrian classes with a sore backside and a punctured bicycle. He gave me a lift in his car, and we chatted while all my thoughts were on the breakfast, which I was going to miss. Maybe he, too, realised it and took me home, where I was served a gourmet South Indian breakfast. We chatted as we ate, and then he dropped me off at my squadron in his staff car.

He could tell that my talents were better suited to more scholarly pursuits and, unbeknown to me, called up my father to convey his feelings about my future. My father, an engineer with the Indian Railways, knew it all along and needed very little convincing. He boarded the next train from Chennai to Pune, was received at the railway station, and was driven to the NDA. I met him in the Commandant's office. Apparently, they had already discussed the path ahead for me. The Commandant brusquely asked me to take a seat and explained to me how I was more suited to more cerebral pursuits.

His words were music to my ears. The soles of both my feet had blisters, my left shin bone had a stress fracture, my right hip bone screamed in pain, and rats were pole-vaulting in my tummy. I was suffering a state of near exhaustion due to the physical exertion and lack of sleep. I could walk straight only because the pain in my left shin bone and the right hip bone balanced each other out. In my condition, I needed no convincing, and, looking at him, I nodded and said, "Sir, I shall abide by your advice because subjects like mathematics and physics interest me more than PT and drill."

My father appeared relieved. He was expecting me to mount a strong defence towards staying put in the Academy. Leaving the Academy of my own volition meant that my father had to shell out a lot of his hard-earned money to reimburse the cost of training that I had undergone, and I promised him to return the whole amount in due course.

Within a week, I was homeward bound, and once I was there, I didn't have to wait over my future plans for long.

During my 12th grade, I aced the Maths World Olympiad. Subsequently, a number of universities like MIT and Caltech offered me admission with full scholarships, but I opted to join the NDA. Now, I needed to get in touch with them, which I did, and both opened their doors for me.

I chose Caltech over MIT: why, one would ask because MIT was numero uno amongst technical institutes. My father has a Bengali friend, a scientist with a number of patents to his name. After graduating from IIT Kharagpur, he opted for Caltech for his master's and doctoral studies and never regretted his decision. He had advised me to join Caltech if I ever decided to study abroad, as it provided a better academic environment and had an excellent faculty for Pure Mathematics, my favourite subject and my first love.

My admission to Caltech was a cakewalk. I landed on the western shores of America in the fall of 2010 and immediately fell in love with the place at first sight, not to mention the faculty and library.

I pursued maths with all my passion. While the faculty was extremely supportive and encouraging, the library became my second home. With zero distractions of booze, grass, and girls, I was in a state of academic Nirvana. I thought, spoke, ate, and slept figures, theorems, and theories. In a record time of six years, I completed my doctoral thesis and started teaching at Caltech with plans to simultaneously continue with my postdoctoral studies. I had been approached by Microsoft, Google, and IBM to join them, but I demurred. WAP contacted me later and asked me to help them in their R&D wing while I continued with my educational pursuits. The pay package offered was beyond my wildest expectations. I joined them in 2017.

As time went by, I became more deeply involved in company affairs and became the 'go-to' man for surmounting seemingly impossible challenges. One of the reasons for my success was the support system around me. There were quite a few South Indians working at WAP, and between us, we ensured mouth-watering vegetarian South Indian fare with curd and rice at the end of every meal. With saatvik food nourishing my stomach, my mind could focus on complex issues. With no distractions of flesh and spirit, my high was conquering the near-impossible issues thrown at me.

Chapter 2

The Team

On 4th March 2020, I received a call from Mike, the Chief Technical Officer (CTO) of WAP. "He said, "Vidya, POTUS has instructed POWAP to develop a solution for the Wuhan virus as quickly as possible, and POWAP has chosen you to lead the effort." I told him that I was honoured to be selected to develop a solution and would like to develop it before the Big Apple loses more people than there are in San Marino, for which I would need a team of bright nerds. "Already done," was Mike's response, "I have contacted Sonny Gill, Aashiq Ali, and Husn Li, and they are on their way and should be with you within 15 minutes. Let me know if you need any other help or resources. And do keep me posted on the progress on a daily basis. Wishing you success."

I had just fifteen minutes to read up their individual profiles before they trooped in; all of them, as per their profiles, were in their late twenties, well-qualified, talented, and high achievers.

Sonny appeared to be the quintessential all-American. Tall, well-built, with sparkling blue eyes, blond silky hair, and a heartwarming, mischievous smile. He majored in Communications and Information Technology, with a focus in Biotechnology. I immediately understood why Mike had chosen him for the team. Reflexively, my lips rounded, and I whistled softly—my reaction to connecting any set of dots, which tends to make people a tad bit uncomfortable. I had tried to curb this habit, but failed.

It turns out that Aashiq Ali was born in Mudrike, near Lahore, Pakistan.

Incidentally, Mudrike is also the headquarters of the infamous Lashkar-e-Taiba (also known as Jamaat-ud-Dawa), a fundamentalist Islamist organization. They have openly declared their hostile agenda toward India and Hindus, with the ultimate goal of achieving Ghazwa-e-Hind (though, of course, this is wishful thinking). I admire Pakistan's panache; not many newly formed nations have had such a rough ride. They lost half of their territory after the Bangladesh Liberation War, while the other half (Baluchis, Sindhis, Pathans, Bantus, and Baltis) continues to resist the Pakistani establishment. Despite all this, a Pakistani Punjabi Mussalmaan takes it in stride, sneering at Indians and labeling them as wimps—good only for Bollywood-style singing and dancing around trees and developing softwares.

A Pakistani Mussalmaan, he firmly believes, is mightier than ten of us. Some may term it as delusion, cheeky, or downright foolhardy, but I feel that the Pakistani Mussalmaan is supremely confident and witty but clever by half.

Back to Aashiq, who, after graduating from Government College, Lahore, studied at MIT for two years, earning a Master's degree in Global Economy before joining WAP.

He is all of 5 feet and 8 inches, his thick hair parted in the centre like most Pakistani cricket stars, and his command of the English language, I guess, is based on mental translation: mentally form the sentence in Urdu and then translate it into English and write it down. But man, his brain, as per his profile, ticks like nobody's business. One of his colleagues, whom I spoke with for a minute, quipped that he is always trying to speak faster and faster, most of it incoherent, and finally, he starts keying in his thoughts on his laptop, which is easier for everyone to follow. He is also a Namaazi, praying five times a day as any devout Muslim would. .

About Husn Li; she is shrouded in mystery. Five feet five inches tall, straight black hair falling to her shoulders, inscrutable face and uncharacteristic almond-shaped eyes, more akin to Tibetans. Born and brought up in China, Husn chose to pursue her education in the US post her schooling. She studied at Caltech so I rang up one of her batchmates whom I knew.

As per her batchmate, Husn appeared to be slow in comprehending initially, maybe because she was accustomed to figures as alphabets, but she came out tops in lateral thinking and problem-solving. Husn was outgoing and sociable with her colleagues, she nonetheless maintained a no-nonsense reputation. Rumour had it that she came from a very poor peasant family in Wuhan province and had a traumatic childhood. Her academic performance at school forced her teachers to take notice, and she was sent to a school of high IQ children in Beijing on scholarship. Her performance there, again rumoured, earned her a scholarship from the Communist Party of China to study at Caltech. However, I did not come across her on campus. Maybe she was not one to frequent the library often.

She is two years older than me and joined WAP last year, sidestepping from google.

THE FIRST MEETING

I was barely done profiling my new team when they walked into the office in t-shirts and jeans. Sonny wore his sandals, Aashiq his Peshawar jootis, and Husn in her Nike sneakers. Sonny was all smiles, Aashiq brooding and Husn poker-faced. She turned out to be a head-turner: her complexion was peach and cream, and her eyes deep, inviting cesspools. If she had desired it, I'm certain the three of us would have vied for her attention, eager to become her friends—or perhaps something even closer. I had a nagging feeling that she knew that she could get menfolk to follow her like puppies. I quickly made a mental note not to look into her eyes directly and steer clear of her during non-working hours. Those eyes could really pied-piper you.

"Welcome, guys," I greeted them in my clipped English with a beaming smile, "to the 'A' Team of WAP," and I quickly made up a ditty and recited: "We at WAP cover the gap."

Between what is and could be.

Daily, we go about our jobs, nay, art, gaily.

Ensuring every piece of our art is sought.

To improve the lot

Of Humanity

And in the instant case.

Increase their Immunity.

I saw them all smile; it was the 'immunity' bit at the end, I guess. I knew that the first meeting would be stormy given the sharp minds and different personalities, so I wanted it to be light-hearted and freewheeling:

"Guys," I said, "we have been asked to develop a Coronavirus Killer Application within a week." There was a collective gasp from all three of them at the tight timelines. "We can do it, guys," I said. "We all know that it will be a year or more before an effective vaccine is developed to combat the Coronavirus, but our collective brains should be able to work out a solution within the next seven days." I then requested comments along with a brief introduction.

Sonny was first off the blocks. "Wuhan Virus or Chinese virus, I would say," he drawled and continued, "let's not beat around the bush, but call a spade a spade. I am an average American guy, simple, honest, and hardworking. Additionally, I have a very high IQ with matching sincerity. I think we Americans have been too nice to the world, especially China. Clearly, China has played the US against Russia while initially appearing to be meek and subservient to the US. In the process, it sought and got cutting-edge US technologies in successive waves. It is well documented in 'the hundred years marathon'. In my opinion, POTUS has done the right thing by tightening the screws on China."

Husn raised her hand to speak, and I nodded. She let off a tirade against the POTUS, saying that he was driving the whole world backwards with his protectionist policies, and that with all the power at his command, he was going to ensure that America never becomes great again. China believed in a peaceful rise and had enough problems of its own, like poverty and illiteracy, to wrest the superpower status from the United States of America. I sensed the undercurrents but kept quiet.

Suddenly, Aashiq lifted his droopy eyelids and said that both the US and China were trying to outsmart each other, but Pakistan was handling them both with aplomb. He added that while both countries wanted Pakistan to be a puppet in their hands, Pakistan got both of them to dance to its tunes while making India look like an anti-Islam bully eager to add more real estate to its territory.

Sonny looked askance at Vidya Sagar, expecting him to let loose a torrent of accusative volleys at Pakistan and Aashiq, but he kept quiet with a smile playing on his face. Suddenly, it struck Sonny that Vidya Sagar was purposely letting the storm brew so that, as a project team, they could go through the classical storming-forming-norming stages before becoming a performing team. Sonny also realised that they didn't have the time to go through the stages sequentially and needed to start delivering as a team quickly. "Cut it, guys," he said, "it's time we started to focus on the task at hand; we only have a week to find a solution."

It was here that Vidya interjected. He said that he agreed with Sonny and added that he would like Sonny to be the Project Lead if there were no objections. There was an eerie silence in the room. None of them was expecting such an announcement. After a short while, they looked at each other and nodded in agreement.

Sonny realised why Vidya had pulled this rabbit out of his hat; he had probably figured that the Chinese and the Pakistani will never accept him as a leader, given the relations between their countries and he, Sonny, would be more acceptable. To overcome the embarrassing silence, Sonny laughed out loud, and with a twinkle in his eyes, he looked at Vidya and said, "It appears that the potato is too hot for you, but I will gladly be the Project Lead."

Taking charge, Sonny told the team that there was no time to waste and laid out the plan. "We have seven days starting now," he said, "by the 24th of April 2021, we have to have a comprehensive solution to Coronavirus: this is the end state we are looking at. I believe that if we examine the virus's origins, causes, and spread patterns, we'll be on the right track. We should also look at the preventive, prophylactic, and therapeutic measures taken by various countries. Finally, we must consider the positive and negative effects, as well as the development of a vaccine as a potential antidote. The four of us are amongst the best brains in the world, so I recommend that each one of us work on the challenge independently, with close collaboration on data collection, expert opinion/advice and, as importantly, providing much-needed breaks through music, meditation, and team activities."

"Your workplace could be this office, with our R&D lab and libraries across the country as input and data providers. Husn may look at China and obtain all the necessary inputs. Similarly, Aashiq could do the same for Europe and Vidya for the rest of Asia. I shall cover the US, and we can address Africa if time permits, as the virus has not yet affected that region. We will all meet at 17:00 hours starting today to share, collaborate, discuss, and debate all issues related to the virus. To help our minds remain fresh and creative, I shall provide some mind-blowing music, Vidya will guide us through meditation, and Husn and Aashiq will together plan some short-duration fun games."

The moment Sonny thanked them for hearing him out and sought queries from them, he noticed Aashiq perk up with a grin at the mention of Husn and him teaming up for fun games and an open, appreciative smile from Husn aimed at Sonny. Sonny sighed inwardly: Aashiq likes Husn, but Husn has eyes for Sonny, and Sonny is not available to the fairer sex!

Why did Husn like Sonny? His striking looks, commanding presence, and flawless etiquette, Sonny was the kind of person most girls found irresistible. But he was oriented toward same-sex relationships. While most of the girls ended up as his friends, a lingering sense of disappointment stayed with them, leaving them to wonder what might have been!

AASHIQ ALI

"What a lucky stroke," thought Aashiq, "Husn and I are in one team!" He knew that Husn in Urdu meant more than just beauty. It would probably include sexy and hot with a haughty, innocent smile playing on the lips. Husn, Aashiq thought to himself, had everything—except the smile. She was always serious with a deadpan face and a discouraging body language.

Aashiq, a born and incurable romantic, decided to romance Husn at the first opportunity to help her out of her serious self. The thought of romancing Husn spurred Aashiq's mind into a self-descriptive journey at a speed faster than light, "Aashiq means lover and Aashiqui nee 'Loving' is in my blood.

It has got to do a lot with the region that I hail from, Punjab. Even though there are two Punjabs today, one on the Indian and the other on the Pakistani side, the stock of people is the same. However, today, they are separated by religious hatred, partition atrocities, and nationalistic jingoism. A Punjabi is hot-blooded, large-hearted and loud by nature. They carry their hearts on their sleeves, and to top it, my parents christened me Aashiq— lover— so I had no choice but to be one.

I am sure my rakish looks and irresistible charm will help me win over Husn's heart, though the Chinese, like most others, are slightly wary of us. Our popular image is of an opiated, drugged jehadi who can't wait to blow himself up to avail the seventy-two 'hoors' (fairies) waiting for him in paradise. I have a bone to pick with this image; it is gender discriminatory: why is this promise only for the male gender, why not seventy-two Adonis for female jehadis?"

Next, his mind took off to the Chinese, "While Husn is extremely beautiful and attractive, privately, we view the Chinese as dog-eating, slit-eyed, foul-smelling, slimy dumb heads whom we have to suck up to because they are our all-weather friends. They cover our back in most sticky situations, but it's not out of charity; they are happy with the Pakistani millstone around the Indian neck and want it to stay that way.

Aashiq is shaken out of his thoughts as they break for coffee, and Husn looks towards him. He quickly pours coffee for her as they move to a side and hands it over. Husn mumbles a thank you and, brusquely, says, "Aa Sick (Aashiq), please come to my office after finishing your coffee." And… she walks away… "What cheek," thinks Aashiq, as he notices the barely concealed disdain in her eyes while talking to him, but he quickly blames it on the image that the world has of the Pakistanis and resolves to win her heart come what may.

HUSN FU LI

As Husn walked away towards her office, she was lost in her thoughts. She had noticed the infatuation in Aashiq's eyes and wanted to nip it in the bud. While she thought highly of Aashiq, her reason for keeping him at a distance was entirely different. She wondered how the team would react if she told them her life story. Knowing that it was fraught with great risk, she decided against it but imagined it anyway.

"I'm a simple mountain girl who was born in a small hamlet outside Lhasa to a Tibetan Buddhist family. We were a poor but honest, fun-loving, and God-fearing family.

My mother was working in the fields when her water broke. Her co-workers made her lie down on a tarpaulin sheet and asked her to push hard. She complied with their instructions, and in a matter of minutes, I was out of her womb, cleaned and wrapped in a Yak hair blanket. She was put on a yak, and we both came home to a stone hut with a kitchen in the centre where smoked yak and lamb meat hung in thin strips, and yak milk toffees ('shurpi') were kept in a bowl. My mother breastfed me while she gobbled down a large bowl of Thukpa, soupy noodles with meat and vegetables. I cradled in her arms and slept. We were close to the kitchen fire so that we could be comfortably warm, while our Tibetan Mastiff dog, Kali, with silken black hair, kept guard next to the door."

"How do I know so much of my first day of birth? My younger brother, Karma, was born four years later. My mother told me I was born in exactly the same way, in the same fields, with Kali keeping guard even then.

"I was named Dolma, another name for Tara, a Buddhist goddess, and started going to the local school about three kilometres away from our home. My father would make us, three school-going children, sit on a Tibetan pony and drop us at the school, while mother would be up before sunrise, get the fire going, clean up the house, till the vegetable patch in our backyard, take out milk and give us some of it to drink, as we headed to our school. My parents both worked in the fields and would get dog-tired by the end of the day, but they were tough as nails, with a stoic countenance. We would all pray in the evening, reciting our Buddhist chants and burning incense in front of the statue of Lord Buddha."

"I liked my school. We had two teachers and fifty-odd students. It was up to class five, and then those students who wanted to pursue further studies had to go to Lhasa. I would be all attention in my class and would tuck every educative nugget into my tiny brain. Always curious to know more, my mind worked extra time to take in most of the learning in the first instance itself. By the time I passed Class V, I had seen births in fields and deaths at home. I had given my father a helping hand in the birth of lambs and foals and helped him bury an old ox. I remember overhearing my parents making love as we all slept in the same room."

"So when I reached Lhasa with my father to take the entrance test for admission to Class VI, I was quite mature for my age and took the test with all seriousness. I completed it in half the stipulated time and scored a perfect 100. My father, aware of my academic abilities, had already arranged for me to stay in Lhasa. However, unbeknownst to us all, fate had different plans for me."

"The Han people rule China, and nurse ambitions to rule the world. They are a Mongoloid East Asian ethnic group native to China. They have ruled China since 206 BC in one form or another. They started as a small community around the Yellow River and then spread outwards to subjugate fifty-five other ethnicities in modern China. They were cold-blooded, cunning, and ruthless, with no ethics or empathy for other beings. That's why they have no compunction in killing and eating rats, cats, bats, and whatever else that swims, flies, or walks! Tibetans are different people ethnically. We have our own language, culture, and customs. The Chinese have been able to subjugate us and have forced us to dance to their tune."

"The Han Chinese follow a 'Bright Student Development Programme', where children of other ethnicities, especially Tibetans, with very high IQs, are brought to Beijing and admitted to one of the government-run schools. They are provided with a new name, free education and boarding, and regular classes are conducted to mould them into Han Chinese.

Over time, most students convert and become proselytisers for converting their own ethnic communities into Han Chinese. Confucius once said, 'The best win is without fighting', and, over time, the Hans achieved their goals without firing a shot. However, when these methods fall short, they can be ruthless, as seen in Xin Xiang province, where they are subjugating the Uighur Muslims through unlawful and inhumane means."

"So, as part of the Han plan, I was told to pack my bags and move to Beijing. My life would now be dictated by the Chinese government as I waved my parents goodbye and boarded the Z22 train to Beijing. Forty-one hours later, I arrived at the Beijing station and was taken to the Yellow Chrysanthemum Scholars Academy, a government-run school for academically high-performing students. About 90 percent of the students in my class were Hans, proportional to their population in China. Interestingly, they are also the largest ethnic minority, eighteen percent, in the world with a little less than 200,000 in India, of all the places."

"The Chinese Communist government, over time, has inculcated discipline and unquestionable obedience in its people, and so was the case with my classmates. I was made to feel comfortable right from day one. My dormitory was spartan but spotlessly clean, the food was bland but nutritious, and the school was competitive but friendly.

Within a month, I stopped missing home and started liking my new life with Baidu as my teacher to answer all my questions and queries, within and outside the school curriculum. I also started mastering the Chinese language and developed an interest in Chinese calligraphy. We, the world roofers, are quiet people who can be in good company for hours without speaking. I grew quieter and more perceptive, realizing that I could easily handle my class syllabus, just as I had in my village school. I used my self-study time to learn the Class VII material and unsurprisingly, topped my class. Half-jokingly, I told my teacher that I could pass the Class VII exam as well. The teacher, a matronly Han, decided to test me and handed me the full set of Class VII exams. I completed them and thought nothing more of it, assuming she was joking. By then, I was already looking forward to going home for the holidays."

"I travelled on the same train back to Lhasa. My father received me at the station, and we rode on horses to our home in the village. At home, my mother, Karma, and my cousins were waiting eagerly for my return. We shared hugs, enjoyed a hearty meal, and danced late into the night. As we slept on the floor next to the kitchen fire, snuggled against each other, I realised how much I missed the clean air, the starlit sky, Buddhist chants, smoked meat, and Yak milk. From the next morning onwards, I helped my mother with her daily chores. My father insisted that we have our morning and evening meals together. In the morning, it was Thupka, and in the evenings, cereal gruel. I had so much to tell about my life at school and in Beijing—how everything felt different, even better. The malls, the cars, the fashion, the restaurants, the movies—it was a whole new world."

"On the third day of my vacation, my father asked me to help him in the fields. While we worked, he explained to me the Han Chinese strategy of 'winning without fighting."

"My father explained they indoctrinate the best minds, shaping them into the Han way of thinking. This gradually leads to assimilation of ethnic minorities into Han culture, without coercion or violence—unless necessary. They have committed genocides in the past against the Tibetans, they are now using similar tactics with the Uighur Muslims. China calls the Dalai Lama a murderer and plans to supplant him with its choice after he dies. Slowly, the world will forget about Tibet as an independent country which was annexed by China. We will lose our identity, culture, and religion. We will be like Hans. I was deeply shaken by his words. and promised my father that I would always keep in mind that I am a Tibetan and would work to free Tibet from the clutches of the Chinese."

"Together, my father and I decided that I should change my name to sound more like a Han, become a member of the Communist Party of China, work hard to rise up in its ranks with an aim to become the Minister of Foreign Affairs and then influence the world's opinion in a manner that the world applies enough pressure forcing China to relent. We knew that it wasn't a cakewalk, but it had to be done before we could stop and reverse the Chinese road roller."

"I returned from the vacation to find that I had been promoted to Class VIII, as I had scored straight 'A's' in the Class VII test that I took. I was marked out as a child prodigy. In Class X, I changed my name from Dolma to Husn Fu Li, and after topping the Class XII examinations countrywide, I was told to apply for admission into MIT.

I did that and flew to the US for my higher studies, but not before joining the Communist Party of China. I was told that the party and the country are supreme, and one should always be loyal to them. I was also to give a monthly report to the party on my activities in the US. In a sense, I was to have a handler the moment I landed on the US shores. I was prepared for it, having moulded myself into a Han Chinese, with my love for China being second to none. My official strategy was to get the best education, work in a cutting-edge technology firm and then return to China to exploit my technical knowledge to further Chinese national interests."

In all the briefings before my departure, I noticed most men getting attracted to me. It was different from the school boys' tomfoolery. I wasn't caught off guard. When I returned home after Class X, my mother had already warned me that my beauty would draw the attention of many men, some of whom might make advances. She told me to view my youth and beauty as powerful assets— never outright rejecting their attention, but never fully yielding either. In doing so, she said, they would remain captivated and do anything to win my favour."

So, I fluttered my eyes at each one of these guys and noted their contact details. They are all in touch with me, as are my American contacts, and here I am, a double doctorate, 25-year-old virgin beauty being pursued by many but succumbed to none. A couple of them tried to push their advances, but my Kung Fu training—I'm a black belt—served me well. The black eyes I gave them acted as a strong deterrent to the others."

SWIMMING WITH SHARKS

Before Husn could continue further, Aashiq landed up in her office unannounced and excited. "Look, Husn," he said, "I am already onto the broad contours of a preventive solution, but I need your guidance to work the whole thing out."

Ignoring Aashiq's dreamy looks, Husn told him to get hold of the other two so that all of them could listen in and take it further. They decided to meet in Sonny's office and asked Vidya to join them.

Sonny was busy on his laptop when they reached his office. Before he could speak, Aashiq, all excited, told him that he was already on the broad contours of the solution, which was more preventive than remedial. Husn butted in to say that they should be looking at both preventive and remedial aspects to provide a holistic solution. Suddenly, Vidya's lips rounded, and he started whistling softly. The rest of them looked askance at him. With an awkward smile, he quickly explained the unintended whistling and what had sparked it. His idea was to develop an app that could navigate like a driverless car, avoiding the virus along the way. Everyone seemed to warm up to the concept, but Sonny pointed out that it would only solve half the problem—the preventive aspect. A remedy also needed to be developed.

As Aashiq mentioned that pharmaceutical companies could work on remedies better, Sonny's mobile rang; it was Mike, the COO, calling. He excused himself and went out to take the call. As he moved out, Husn's mobile rang, and it was a member of the Politburo Standing Committee calling. Her expression remained unreadable as she politely excused herself and stepped out to take the call. Yet, inside, her mind was in turmoil: why would someone from the highest, most powerful committee of the CCP be calling her? Aashiq almost got up to follow Husn outside but controlled the sudden urge and instead got into an animated discussion with Vidya.

Husn returned to the room a little earlier than Sonny, who came in a couple of minutes later. Sonny was buzzing with excitement as he shared the details of a call from Mike about his recent meeting with POTUS. During their one-on-one discussion at the White House, the President revealed credible intelligence suggesting that China had deliberately betrayed both the US and Europe with the Wuhan Virus. Mike had informed Sonny that POTUS disclosed how the Wuhan Virology Institute (WVI) had developed the virus, conducting experiments on bats with a $3.7 million grant from the US government, approved by the National Institutes of Health (NIH).

New intelligence now suggests that the virus was a biological strike orchestrated by China, with assistance from Russia. To confirm these findings and find an antidote, POTUS tasked the team with tracing the virus back to its origin at the Wuhan Virology Institute (WVI).

He believed that the presence of the Chinese woman would facilitate their entry, as all foreign nationals were currently barred from the institute.

According to POTUS's intelligence, Russia had actively assisted China in executing the biological strike in Europe. One of the attacks was believed to have occurred during Game Zero in Italy. While Russia reported a high number of infections, the surprisingly low fatality rate suggested a cover-up. POTUS insisted that Russian involvement be thoroughly confirmed as well.

After narrating the entire story to his team, Sonny asked for their thoughts. Aashiq was the first to respond, saying that investigating the virus's source and Game Zero was beyond their expertise, and they should focus on developing the app. Husn and Vidya agreed, but Sonny reminded them that POTUS's instructions left no room for refusal. The discussion, he said, should focus on how best to accomplish the task.

Again Aashiq was the first one to speak as he suggested that the origin of the virus and the suspected strike should be investigated by sub-teams of two each. As others nodded in agreement, he added that Husn and he were best suited for WVI as the Chinese would view him, a Pakistani, in favourable light. Aashiq's suggestion was reasonable, but Husn raised her hand and said she was willing to take up the challenge—provided Sonny accompanied her. Aashiq, looking disappointed, turned to Vidya, silently pleading for his support.

Vidya's lips rounded, and he started whistling softly. All of them turned towards him, rolled their eyes and waited for him to say something. Smiling to hide his embarrassment, Vidya came to Aashiq's help and said that the Russian angle could be best covered by Sonny because he could read and write Russian, and the Chinese would definitely view Aashiq more favourably compared to Sonny.

Vidya suggested, "Sonny and I team up and travel to Amsterdam to verify the information provided by POTUS. Amsterdam, he explained, is a magnet for European tech enthusiasts due to its reputation for weed and sex. In today's world, he added, nothing happens without the black hats being aware of it."

Sonny agreed and suggested that they could also visit the San Siro Stadium for a look, as it wasn't far from Amsterdam. He called out to Husn and said that her team would need to work out a way to investigate WVI.

Unlike Sonny, Husn did not share the details of the call she had received from the member of the Politburo Standing Committee. She had met him only once earlier in Beijing, just before she left for her studies in the US. In fact, he had spoken to her on behalf of the Committee, a kind of pep talk, to help her excel in her higher education and report anything interesting and important in the monthly briefing. He had shared his mobile number and said that in case of something really important, she could ping him anytime. He had a piercing gaze that unsettled Husn. She got a feeling that he was taken in by her youthful charm and, given half a chance, would force himself on her. Husn shuddered within, got up quickly, bowed, and left the meeting.

Now, as Husn had returned his call, he asked her to call him back on VOIP. Husn complied, and Kun Kar Li, as he was called, got straight to the point. He acknowledged her decision to inform her Beijing guardian about her current project and then told her that her assistance was needed for a national mission concerning the virus. As Husn expressed her eagerness, he explained that while many countries were blaming China for the virus's origin, there were growing indications that it could have been a biological strike by a global power aimed at crippling China.

The party leadership, he said, needed to investigate further. Although the virus had been developed at the Wuhan Virology Institute (WVI), scientists from thirty-two countries, including the US, had been working there. This raised the possibility that one or more of these scientists could have unintentionally or intentionally released the virus in Wuhan.

Kun Kar also conveyed that, due to her background at Caltech and WAP, along with her loyalty and commitment to the party, she had been chosen to visit the Wuhan Virology Institute and conduct an investigation to confirm or refute these claims. Officially, her task would be to carry out a physical and cybersecurity audit, thus serving two purposes—her report would not only assess security but also put an end to the conspiracy theories surrounding China's involvement in the virus's release. "As importantly," replied Husn, "My report would be more acceptable to the world because of my Caltech and WAP background." "Bang on," said Kun Kar, promising her all the help in the investigation, including security clearance for WVI, before hanging up.

Sonny's question about whether she would be comfortable teaming up with Aashiq snapped her out of her thoughts. She nodded in agreement, though she couldn't help wondering how best to dampen Aashiq's ardor. Aloud, she told Sonny that she was confident about organising their visit to WVI; Kun Kar's call and his promise of help were, to Husn's mind, master keys to all the communist doors in China.

Meanwhile, Vidya realised that they would need to be in touch all the time and worked out an arrangement with DARPA. "Guys," he said, "we would need to stay in communication with each other 24/7, whether on land, in the air, or underwater. Each of us will have a nanochip embedded between our left jaw and ear. This will connect us via a network of geostationary satellites, and the chips will be undetectable by metal detectors or x-ray machines. Additionally, our conversations will remain secure, with no one else able to access them."

Sonny nodded at Vidya in appreciation and continued with his briefing. "While at Amsterdam or Wuhan," he said, "we have to be discreet in our enquiries, and if, at any time, the situation appeared life-threatening, they were to abort the mission and return to the USA."

"We'll be traveling for long hours across multiple time zones, so avoiding jet lag is crucial. To stay in top form, we need to hydrate well, sleep as much as possible, eat light and healthy, and avoid smoking and drinking. Our departure from the US will be via Air Force transport: Vidya and I will fly directly to Amsterdam, while Husn and Aashiq will fly separately to Singapore, from where they'll catch a connecting flight to Beijing."

"The whole investigation will be recorded in the nanochip, which is activated through brain signals. It will also save all visual evidence in auto-generated folders. The chip is a marvel developed through Artificial Intelligence, and all the data collected in the chips can also be transferred to my computer here in the US, again through brain signals." Sonny's mobile rang, and he excused himself; the call lasted barely thirty seconds. The voice on the other end informed me that the US Air Force would have two aircraft ready within the hour. Sonny told them to pack and reach the cafeteria in the next 30 minutes to grab a bite before explaining.

The food at the cafeteria was a delight for Sonny and Husn with ham, pork, chicken, and fish on offer and a nightmare for Aashiq and Vidya because Aashiq could eat only halal meat, and he did not like fish, while Vidya was a vegetarian.

Sonny and Husn moved ahead to pick up their plates and served themselves from the food counters. As Sonny walked ahead, Husn observed his subtle movements and instinctively sensed that he was not interested in women. She couldn't help but sigh at the collective loss to womankind. A sudden urge to strike up a conversation with him took hold—he seemed like such a genuine person, and possibly a good friend. She gently took him by the elbow and led him to a table for two, while Vidya and Aashiq settled at a nearby table, indulging in large portions of salad and cheese.

As they sat down, Sonny looked at Husn, and her eyes told him that she knew; he was both happy and relaxed. He told her that they could now focus completely on working out a qualitatively much superior model to combat the virus without any distractions. Husn nodded and, softly covered his hand with her own, added that they would be very good friends too. They finished their dinner, gathered their bags, and made their way to the main office foyer, preparing to head to the air force station.

As they trooped into the main foyer, it was 00:30 hours. There were two cars waiting for them. Sonny called all of them into the small restroom near the reception, inserted the nanochip in them with the help of disposable syringes, and asked Vidya to do the same for him. Just a prick, and the millimetre chip was implanted in all of them. Sonny checked with all to see if it was successfully implanted and, upon hearing a yes and seeing two nods of the head, told them that the chips also have a built-in blockchain system, which would come in very handy.

Suddenly, raising her hands, Husn said, "Please give me two minutes of your time." Initially, she chose not to share the details of Kun Kar Li's call with her team. However, she decided it was best to come clean, realizing that sooner would be better than later.

In her low and measured tone, she informed the team that she had received a call from Kun Kar Li, a member of the highest and most powerful Chinese Communist Committee. She was tasked by him to carry out an audit of the Wuhan Virology laboratory as they, the Chinese, suspected that the spread of the virus was a deliberate act of sabotage, which needed to be confirmed or negated. She also told the team about herself: from birth to her education, name change, and monthly reporting to her handler in China.

Suddenly, Vidya's lips rounded, and he started whistling. The rest of them looked askance at him, and his cheeks reddened in acute embarrassment. With a sheepish grin, he said, "There's an old Chinese curse: 'May you live in interesting times.' It seems that we are on the brink of entering such a phase ourselves. Both countries suspect each other of initiating the pandemic, and now, as software warriors at WAP, we've been tasked with the responsibility of confirming or dispelling these suspicions for both sides. We have been thrown into the deep end of the pool, which may have killer sharks in it. I firmly believe that only our sharp brains and excellent software skills will keep us afloat and clear of the sharks." Aashiq sighed inwardly as he silently agreed with Vidya and wondered why the hell he was getting into this mess. He got his answer as he glanced towards Husn.

Sonny was eager to relay details of Husn's conversation with Kun Kar Li to PROWAP but held back, as Husn indicated that, in turn, she would be obligated to inform Kun Kar Li about the change in the team's tasking—potentially putting the Sonny–Vidya team under Chinese scrutiny.

They got into two cars, Vidya and Sonny leading and Husn and Aashiq following in the second car. The ride to the aircraft was brief, and they boarded at 01:15 hours. As the sole passengers, they watched as the pilots, already waiting on the tarmac, entered their cockpits and began preparing the aircraft for takeoff.

Aashiq gallantly offered to carry Husn's rucksack into the aircraft, but she refused. Aashiq, not being the one to give up, got her a coke and inquired if she needed anything else. By now, Husn had realized that Aashiq was head over heels in love with her. Although she felt no romantic interest, she appreciated his brilliance and generous heart. She decided to talk with him later, as she needed to make an important call before the aircraft began taxiing.

She took out her mobile and dialled Kun Kar Li's number. It was late afternoon in Beijing and Kun Kar Li was in a meeting. When he saw Husn's name flashing on his mobile screen, his pulse raced. Excusing himself from the meeting, he stepped into his office to take the call. His greeting in Mandarin came out as more of a croak, leaving him frustrated by the effect Husn had on him.

Husn, in her business-like tone, conveyed that her company had agreed to her request to visit WVI, and she was already on a US Air Force aircraft bound for Singapore along with Aashiq. Kun Kar was sceptical about Aashiq but relaxed when Husn told him that Aashiq was Pakistani and would do her bidding. Regarding Sonny and Vidya, she told Kun Kar that they had been briefed separately, and she wasn't aware of their tasking.

Kun Kar told Husn that he would charter a flight for her and Aashiq from Singapore to Beijing, and the Chinese Defence Attaché in Singapore would receive and escort them all the way to the chartered flight. Kun Kar also expressed his keenness to meet them in Beijing prior to their onward journey to Wuhan.

As Husn put down her mobile, Aashiq opened his mouth to start a conversation, but she gestured for him to remain silent. Her mind linked with the team through the nano chip. Though her eyes were half-closed, giving the impression of dozing, she transmitted the essence of her conversation with Kun Kar Li through brain signals. Thanks to the blockchain system, her message was instantly received and logged across all the MM chips.

The two aircraft took off within five minutes of each other and were headed for Amsterdam and Singapore, respectively.

HOT RECEPTION

POWAP was a considerate man, and the US ambassador to the Netherlands was a close friend. Knowing that Sonny and Vidya would be alone during their visit, he sent an email to his friend, updating him about the duo's arrival and requesting assistance if necessary. Though the email seemed harmless, it mentioned their planned visit to the San Siro Stadium. The Chinese cyber surveillance unit had been tasked with monitoring any communication that referenced San Siro, so the email was promptly forwarded to the secretary of the Politburo Committee.

The moment the secretary received the email, he sent it to the president and all the members of the committee. The secretary knew that three of the committee members were out of Beijing, so he called up Kun Kar and suggested an urgent meeting with the president. Kun Kar knew that the email needed immediate discussion with President Li Win Ping, and time was of the essence. Asking the secretary to meet him in the president's office, he told his Personal Assistant to set up a meeting with the president, took the elevator to the basement parking, got into his Hongqui L5 Sedan, and drove to the president's office in Zhongnanhai.

He knew that Ping, as Kun Kar addressed him, was in his office, but he also knew that Ping was averse to meeting anyone without an appointment; as the joke went, even his wife had to schedule a night with him in bed! Under normal circumstances, he would have waited for the committee meeting, but he knew that this input was time-critical and Ping needed to be informed ASAP.

On his way, he called Husn to inform her about the email and instructed her to gather more information on Sonny and Vidya's visit to Amsterdam and the San Siro Stadium. He then called Lieutenant General Bin Dan, head of the Dirty Tricks Department, to request intelligence on all the team members.

Kun Kar started tracking the two military aircrafts that had taken off at 01:45 and 01:50 from an air force base on the East Coast. His third call was to the European head of the Ministry of State Security; Kun Kar told him to keep a surveillance team on standby.

Ping was informed of Kun Kar Li's request for an unscheduled meeting by his secretary on the intercom while he was being briefed on the American ship's presence in the South China Sea. Normally, the secretary would not have disturbed Ping during the briefing, but she was aware that Ping and Kun Kar Li had been friends since their young communist party cadre days and enjoyed each other's confidence. As Ping picked up the intercom handset, his face betrayed annoyance at being disturbed during the briefing, but when he heard Kun Kar Li's name, he relaxed. He told the secretary to inform him of Kun Kar's arrival and escort Kun Kar Li to his private antechamber.

The aircraft levelled at 35,000 feet MSL, and Vidya started scrolling through all the news items on the Coronavirus. Its spread had been successfully contained in Wuhan, thus ensuring that the rest of China wasn't affected. The US and Europe were facing the brunt of it. Most countries were importing masks and testing kits from China, some of which were found to be defective.

China was being accused of not reporting the pandemic earlier, hoarding face masks and testing kits, and profit-pricing them. A number of countries were requesting companies to move their businesses out of China. US warships had moved menacingly in the South China Sea as a show of force. Chinese companies had bought stakes in major companies across the world. The pharma giants were in a furious race to produce a vaccine, eyeing profits from the pandemic.

So, what was afoot?" thought Vidya. "Was China involved in the final stages of the hundred-year marathon, with the pretender sensing an opportunity to topple the world's monarch? Or had the pandemic given the US and Europe a chance to exploit the anger against China and weaken it economically, thus delivering a blow to its ambitions? And what was Russia up to?"

Husn's message regarding the email and Kun Kar wanting more details shook Vidya out of his thoughts. As Sonny and Aashiq quizzed Husn about the email, Vidya brain texted, saying that Husn definitely needed to pass some inputs to Kun Kar. It was agreed that Husn could pass on the details of their stay in Amsterdam, and while she called up Kun Kar, Aashiq warned Sonny and Vidya of a hot reception in Amsterdam. As Sonny tried to brush off the warning with humor, Aashiq pointed out that the Chinese Ministry of State Security, their intelligence agency, combined the ruthlessness of the FSA with the competence of the CIA. Vidya nodded in agreement and texted that Sonny and him would devise a strategy to outsmart the Chinese.

After her call with Kun Kar Li, Husn began checking her emails, only to remember an hour later that she had intended to speak with Aashiq. Throughout this time, Aashiq had been pretending to be busy, though he couldn't keep his mind or eyes off her. When their gazes finally met, Husn spoke to him gently, telling him that she recognized the kindness in his heart and had sensed his feelings towards her. She then shared her story with him, beginning with her childhood, the transformation she had undergone, and the ultimate purpose of her life. She explained that while she was just a normal girl who dreamed of loving, marrying, and having children, those desires were currently on hold. For now, she suggested, they could simply be good friends.

Aashiq was crestfallen. He was totally enamoured by her and was confident of winning her love. Husn took his right hand in both her hands and gave him a friendly smile. Suddenly, Aashiq laughed and shook his head in disbelief. Since his childhood, Aashiq told Husn, he had lived up to his name It was the first time he had fallen in love, only to be left heartbroken. Husn expressed her sympathy and reassured him of her friendship.

Aashiq brooded for a couple of minutes, head down and suddenly looked up with a jerk. His face now appeared to be beaming with confidence, and his eyes were twinkling with happiness. He told Husn that he respected her decision and accepted her offer of friendship. "As Punjabis," he said, "we value and honor friendship above all else." He assured her that they would be friends for life and that she could always count on him.

Chapter 3

The Plot Thickens

Kun Kar Li reached the president's office in about 20 minutes, was ushered into the antechamber, and served tea. The president was informed of his arrival, and within a couple of minutes, he was in the antechamber meeting Kun Kar Li, who bowed as soon as he saw the president enter. The president bowed in turn and gave Kun Kar a broad smile. Kun Kar begged forgiveness for seeking a meeting with no advance notice and added that the matter at hand required to be brought to the president's attention immediately.

As the president nodded, Kun Kar Li briefed him on the WAP team and its objectives, as well as on Husn's input regarding the Vidya–Sonny duo's move to Amsterdam to investigate the virus's origins in Europe, specifically their visit to the San Siro Stadium in Milan. As he spoke, he noticed a shadow of concern cross the president's face.

Dan," Kun Kar said to the president, "had already gathered the details on both Vidya and Sonny, and he's on his way to the meeting." Before Kun Kar could finish, there was a polite knock on the door, and Dan entered, bowing deeply. "Come in, Dan," the president called out. "You'd better hear Kun Kar Li's briefing before sharing your insights." Kun Kar Li quickly brought Dan up to speed on the information he hadn't yet received and then inquired about Vidya and Sonny.

Dan looked respectfully at the president and said, "Sir, initially POTUS had asked POWAP to work out a panacea for the virus utilising his brainy software professionals. A team of four persons, Husn, Sonny, Aashiq Ali, and Vidya have been formed and tasked by POWAP. While Vidya was nominated as the lead by POWAP, but within the team, he requested Sonny to take on the mantle of leadership."

"All four of them are academically brilliant with original ideas and look forward to challenges: the tougher, the better. When it comes to their vulnerabilities, Sonny is highly sensitive and tends to swing to extremes, while Aashiq's overconfidence masks the fact that his family in Pakistan is struggling, driving him to seek money through any means possible. Vidya is prideful of his heritage and intellect. As for Husn, she is our own, an invaluable asset in every sense."

Having heard Dan out, President Ping looked at Kun Kar Li. Kun Kar Li knew that the whole story about the virus was known only to five people, and Dan was not one of them. Keeping this in mind, Kun Kar Li suggested that while they had nothing to hide and the Sonny–Vidya team could proceed with their investigations, they should be cautious. Given the Gweilos' (Westerners') tendency to fabricate anti-Chinese narratives, it would be wiser to thwart their efforts. He added that there were two ways of doing so: the subtle way and the direct way.

President Ping looked at Dan and asked for his opinion. Dan started by saying that his men were capable of tackling the Sonny–Vidya team effectively in both ways. In Brussels," he began, "a Chinese family sells handcrafted leather footwear to the wealthy. The shop owner's son, Love Li, is a 24-year-old handsome young man works as our agent. He's a highly trained assassin, capable of using his looks to ensnare people like Sonny. I suggest we use him to distract the team and draw them away from San Siro Stadium.

Kun Kar Li differed with Dan's recommendation and said that the direct way would be a better option as the stakes were very high and no chances could be taken. He suggested that Love Li be tasked to eliminate both Sonny and Vidya and then their bodies disposed off in one of the famous canals of Amsterdam. He completed his argument with a Chinese proverb that a flute couldn't be played if there were no bamboo.

Now, both of them looked at the President, who, instead of making a decision, started musing aloud. He said that the winds blowing across the world were frequently changing directions, and while the Chinese, an ancient civilisation, were working to earn their rightful place in the world, Gweilos viewed their philosophy of 'Peaceful Rise' with trepidation. "Remember," the president stated, "history is always shaped by the victor. The United States, having stifled the growth of nations like Germany and Japan and fractured the USSR into numerous smaller states, presents itself as the champion of the free world.

I am aware that the US fears our peaceful ascent and will go to any lengths to ensure that the 21st century is not the Chinese Century. In the late 1970s, we had chosen to work towards the development of our motherland through the four pillars of modernisation. Forty years later, we are the world's manufacturing hub; we have stakes in most African countries as well as in most of the European multinational giants."

"Our One Road One Belt initiative has been welcomed by almost all the partner countries and our Armed Forces too have modernised into leaner, meaner, and more effective organisations. While the US focuses on trying to make itself great again, it has nearly abdicated its role as the global policeman. It seems likely that in the next 5 to 10 years, we will be welcomed into that position as our economy rises to become the world's largest. However, this is only one side of the story, and we must never underestimate our adversary."

"As Uncle Sam limps through its efforts to become great again, its spy agencies and those of its allies are working overtime to impede our progress through internal strife, sabotage and loss of face. What happened in Hong Kong? How did it suddenly come to a boil? Who fanned the feelings and funded the arson and rioting? And why wouldn't it stop?"

"We are being singled out over COVID-19: at best, we are being blamed for not providing the inputs on the pandemic timely, and at worst, we are being blamed for the COVID-19 breakout in Europe and the USA. Mark my words, in due course, Taiwan, the South China Sea, Tibet, Uighur Muslims in Xin Xiang province and border disputes with India and Vietnam will all raise their ugly heads to hobble and stymie our growth. In the human world, perceptions matter more than reality, and our adversaries will leave no stone unturned to rub our noses in the mud. For these reasons, we do not have the luxury of the subtle option against the Sonny- Vidya duo."

Looking at Dan, he directed that the duo should be eliminated within hours of their arrival at the Schiphol Airport.

"Sir, your orders will be carried out, and both of them will be dead in a couple of hours of their landing," said Dan, and he bowed and moved out of the room. Dan had already decided to call Love Li and put him on the job.

Kun Kar Li complimented the president on his clarity of mind and said that he would oversee this operation personally. President Ping nodded and asked Kun Kar Li to tell Husn to find out the mole in the Wuhan Virology laboratory, which let out the Virus in Wuhan. "I am not buying this bullshit of the virus having originated in the wet market of Wuhan," said the president. Kun Kar Li nodded and replied that he was confident that Husn would be able to get down to the bottom of the mystery of the release of the Coronavirus and provide us with the answers.

As Kun Kar Li bowed to leave, two thoughts crossed his mind: first, it was fortunate that the Westerners suspected a strike only at the San Siro Stadium, while cities like London, New York, Los Angeles, Ohio, and Chicago were not yet on their radar. Two, could there be a third party involved in the release of the virus from the Wuhan Virology laboratory? He was confident that China's famous 'Bat woman', Shi Phengli, who was in charge of all research regarding Coronavirus, was a committed patriot and would not have permitted any leak under her watch Could the Russians be playing us against the Americans and the EU, just as we had done when we seized superpower status from them after the USSR disintegrated?

While driving back to his office, he decided to brief Husn on both the 'bat woman' and the possible Russian role in the release of the virus.

It was around midday in Oslo. The sky was overcast, and an intermittent drizzle since the morning had made the day slightly cooler. The CEOs of the world's three largest pharmaceutical companies were at the Grand Hotel for lunch.

They had taken care to book a corner table, which went unnoticed by most of the diners. With the world fighting the Coronavirus pandemic, their companies were in a race to develop a vaccine. Why were they having lunch together? They could have been on the backs of their research scientists, goading them on to develop the vaccine soonest and maintaining absolute secrecy from the other two companies.

Business management teaches that competition is the best for business because the customer gets the best quality stuff at the best possible price, but these companies do things differently.

Van Dook, CEO of Pfizer, was holding the attention of the other CEOs. "Gentlemen," he said, "every pandemic is a scourge of mankind, and we have a moral responsibility to develop a vaccine as soon as possible to keep everybody alive and healthy. We also have to ensure that pandemics and their ilk keep visiting humankind so that new vaccines and medicines are developed to keep humans safe and healthy and, of course, our companies keep growing financially."

It is important that we provide a vaccine for COVID-19 at the appropriate time and share the formula so that we can fix the price of the vaccine and not undercut each other. Our companies and our shareholders stand to benefit immensely if we time the commercial production and sale of the vaccine right. "You all would be happy to know," he continued, "that our Chinese friends are coming under pressure for not permitting investigations into the origin of the virus or providing its live samples. They have added fuel to the fire of suspicion by denying sharing of inputs on the virus and permitting international flights to and from Wuhan till long after having banned the domestic flights. They are very sensitive to anyone investigating the Wuhan Virology laboratory, and they suit us perfectly."

Before Van could raise his wine glass to propose a toast, Karl, CEO of Novartis, butted in to say that, as per one of his highly placed sources in China, the Chinese president had permitted an investigation team from WAP to visit the WVI. Upon hearing this, a look of concern crossed their faces, and they exchanged worried glances. Karl went on to explain that the WAP team was made up of a Chinese woman and a Pakistani man. While the Chinese source was confident they could manipulate the investigation in their favour—since the Chinese woman was a protege of the Communist Party and the Pakistani man could be easily pressured—Karl, however, believed that the WAP team should be neutralized as soon as possible to eliminate any risk of the vaccine's production and sale.

Norman, CEO of La Roche, agreed with Karl and offered to undertake the neutralisation of the team before they paid a visit to the WVI. He asked Karl to provide their whereabouts to him within an hour. Signalling the end of the meeting, VanDook raised a toast to the vaccine and the rest joined him.

Forty-five minutes later, Norman was given the particulars of the aircraft, the two passengers it was carrying, and its flight plan to Singapore and, from there, to Beijing. Norman passed the details to a Chinese Triad Society, the Big Circle Gang, with instructions to eliminate Husn and Aashiq after they landed at Changi Airport. The gang was to be paid one million dollars, with fifty percent as an advance. An hour later, the full amount was transferred to a bank account in Hong Kong, and a message was received from the gang confirming that the hit would proceed as planned.

Chapter 4

In the Deep End

Love Li received his instructions from Dan via VOIP while eating breakfast at his place in Brussels. After finishing the pork noodle stew, freshly prepared and served by his mother, he made his way to his room.

About 80 years ago, his grandfather had moved out of Shanghai and reached Brussels with his wife, two daughters, and a son. He initially worked as a daily wage earner performing sundry jobs and then started a small shoe shop with a loan. In next to no time, his grandfather realised that he was a naturally gifted shoemaker and started taking orders from the elite of Brussels. He would craft both gents' and ladies' shoes, and his workmanship was both visually attractive and comfortable to wear and walk in. He was a wise man and, unlike others who frittered away their earnings in drinking and gambling, he put his children through school and purchased a small house.

His son, Love Li's father, joined him after completing school and made a name for himself as a shoemaker, too. The two daughters, Love Li's aunts, grew up into beautiful young ladies and married twin Chinese brothers working in France. Love Li's father married a Chinese Belgian girl who used to teach calligraphy at a local school. After Love Li was born, his parents were advised not to have any more children because of his mother's medical condition. Love Li studied in a local school, learned four languages, and earned a black belt in Kung Fu by the time he was 16 years old.

He was spotted by the Chinese Communist Party's recruitment cell and was given a scholarship to study in China. While there, he was trained in basic military skills and drafted into the Chinese Secret Service's Overseas Wing. By the time he turned 22, he was a suave diplomat and a ruthless killer.

He had the looks and the build of Lin Dan, the famous badminton player, minus the moustache, and both ladies and men like Sonny and were naturally attracted to him. He was assigned to the immigration section at the Chinese Embassy in Belgium, but he actually worked for the Chinese Overseas Secret Service. In a short time of two years, he had already carried out four successful hits on high-value targets with no evidence whatsoever. In all his hits, he had injected Ma Huang, an ancient Chinese herbal drug, in high concentration to cause heart failure within an hour of the drug being injected.

After coming into his room, Love Li checked the flight tracker on his mobile. The aircraft carrying Sonny and Vidya was still four hours away. The drive from his place in Brussels to Schiphol Airport would take about two and a half hours. He had to prepare adequate concentration of Ma Huang for two heart failures.

His plan was to accidentally bump into Sonny at the airport and offer them coffee at the Starbucks outlet.

Having been briefed about Sonny, he knew that Sonny would not be able to resist him. He would offer them a lift up to the hotel they would have booked in at Amsterdam. His plan was to take them to a crowded bar and lace their drinks with Ma Huang powder. He would chat with them for about half an hour and then excuse himself as they would collapse any time after that. They would be taken to the hospital, where they would be declared dead, and the post-mortem would indicate heart failure due to a heavy drug overdose.

After preparing the concentrate, Love Li went in for a bath, splashed after-shave lotion on his face, changed, and drove off for Schiphol Airport. The aircraft carrying Sonny and Vidya was still three and a half hours away.

Husn and Aashiq had a long flight ahead, and the attendant advised them to rest, but Aashiq, having overcome the heartbreak, was in one of his inspirational moods. Visibly excited, he was explaining to Husn how he would create an application for mobiles which would detect and kill the virus before it came in contact with the body.

"Let's quickly go through the characteristics of the Wuhan Virus," he told Husn, who looked daggers at him and tried to hit him with the small pillow provided to them by the attendant, as she was keen to have a shut-eye. Shielding himself from the blows, Aashiq told her that the virus is pleomorphic enveloped particles containing single-stranded RNA associated with a nucleoprotein within a capsid comprised of matrix protein. He added that these club-shaped glycoprotein projections are found in mammalian species and seventy percent of the viruses are transferred to humans from other mammals, mostly by bats because they live in communities and travel long distances.

By now, Husn had perked up and was all ears. As Aashiq explained, the transmission of viruses could be directly from bats to humans or through another animal and was usually via airborne droplets to the mucosa. "Post transmission," he said, "the virus replicates locally in cells of the ciliated epithelium causing cell damage and inflammation. However, its life as an airborne droplet in the air or on the ground itself was very short, and because it was vulnerable to heat, he proposed to attack and neutralise the virus when it was most vulnerable by creating heat fields."

"So you are looking to develop an application which will detect Coronavirus in the air or ground and then generate adequate heat to kill it," said Husn. 'Precisely,' replied Aashiq, "I want to prevent it from infecting the human body." "But that's only half the job done; what about the cure after a person is infected?" queried Husn. "That I will leave for Vidya," replied Aashiq, "because he has an in-depth knowledge of Ayurveda, an ancient Indian medical science which helps build the human immune system to fight and neutralise the virus. Vidya will be able to prepare a concoction of various herbs which will develop effective immunity against this ruddy Coronavirus virus and fight it too." Aashiq brain texted the details of his idea to Vidya as he finished explaining it to Husn.

Vidya looked at his watch. Schiphol Airport was two hours away. He sent his reply to Aashiq via brain text, praising his idea for combating the Coronavirus and promising a specially formulated blend of Ayurvedic herbs to counter it.

Signing off from his brain texting conversation with Aashiq, Vidya turned to Sonny and told him of his suspicion that they could be in for a nasty reception at Schiphol Airport and he, Sonny, should request the pilot to land at Eindhoven Airport instead of Schiphol.

Vidya reasoned that Eindhoven was about an hour and a half by road from Schiphol Airport and the reception party at Schiphol would not be able to make it to Eindhoven Airport by the time they landed there and moved on to Amsterdam. Sonny agreed and walked up to the cockpit, where he made his request to the captain, a six-foot-two Texan. The captain drawled, 'Why not, Sonny boy? I'll request it from the ATC; you can stand right here.'

The captain got through to the ATC at Eindhoven Airport and requested a change in the landing plans. To the captain's surprise, the ATC refused his request and instructed him to land at Schiphol Airport, citing heavy traffic at Eindhoven. Unknown to them, Love Li had already foreseen this contingency and spoken to the right people to prevent the aircraft from landing elsewhere other than at Schiphol Airport.

The captain turned around, gave an apologetic look to Sonny, shrugged his shoulders and said, "Sorry, Sonny, I tried, and normally, the ATC would have acceded to my request. They may be having instructions not to permit the landing of our aircraft at Eindhoven Airport for whatever reasons." Sonny was taken aback, but he could think on his feet and look around the corners. "Sir," he said to the pilot, "I strongly suspect that the denial of our request is part of a larger plan to hinder our mission and likely our lives are in danger."

"So, could the captain please organise a powerful car at the tarmac which could take both Vidya and him to Amsterdam through an unmarked exit?" The captain, who was quite cut up because his request was denied, drawled, "Don't worry, lad, I will make sure that you reach Amsterdam in quick time without any bad men harming you." He then sent a coded message to the CIA station chief in Amsterdam, marveling at the technology that made it possible from thirty thousand feet above the Earth. Fortunately, the station chief was also a Texan, and they had been friends since their school days. The decoded message conveyed that the captain was carrying valuable cargo for the station chief, which needed to reach Amsterdam as soon as possible, and it was to be collected personally by him at the tarmac itself. It also gave the aircraft's touchdown time and its location on the tarmac.

The CIA Chief was intrigued by the captain's message; his friend had never before sent him such a message, and he wondered if it was a prank being played on him. But he told himself that his childhood friend, though of ready wit and fertile mind, would never summon him to the tarmac as a lark. Telling himself that there would be a serious enough reason for such a message, he glanced at his watch and realised that he had to leave immediately to reach the airport in time. He picked up his jacket, told his secretary that he would be out for the day, and walked briskly to his Jaguar sports car, a compact and powerful beast with a 5-litre engine.

As he gunned it to life, the car seemed to leap out of the parking, and the station chief smiled, confident that he would be at the tarmac before the aircraft taxied in. En route, he rang up his opposite member in the Dutch Secret Service and coordinated his entry into the airside area of the airport. He was told to enter through gate number eleven, where a pilot vehicle would wait to take him to the aircraft.

Love Li was at Schiphol Airport when he received a message from the DCM of the Chinese embassy in Amsterdam, informing him about the message sent by the captain to the CIA station chief: the station chief's mobile was monitored by the Chinese embassy cyber team, and it picked up the message as it was received by the station chief, but they couldn't get its contents.

Interesting, thought Li, 'why would the captain send a message to the CIA station chief of all the people? First, the request for landing at Eindhoven Airport and now this message by the captain to the CIA station chief'; he decided to go to the ATC and monitor the landing of the aircraft and movement of passengers instead of waiting for them in the immigration area.

The aircraft carrying Sonny and Vidya was to touch down at 16:00 hours local time, and Li was in the ATC with a pair of binoculars at 15:55 hours. The Jaguar sports car, moving at 100 miles an hour, its powerful engine purring under the bonnet, reached gate number 11 as the aircraft touched down. There was a five-minute delay at the gate because of the paperwork, and at 16:05 hours, the pilot's vehicle led it to the aircraft.

Li watched the aircraft touch down and get off the runway towards bay number 35. At 16:10 hours, the aerobridge was firmly connected to the front left door of the aircraft. He calculated that the passengers would start to disembark and head for immigration in another five minutes; he decided to leave immediately so that he would be all set at immigration before the passengers arrived there.

At 16:11 hours, the Jaguar sports car reached the aircraft and the captain, along with Sonny and Vidya, came down using the emergency stairway of the aerobridge. There was no shaking of hands or back-slapping, and everyone had a face mask covering the nose and mouth. The captain introduced Sonny and Vidya to his friend and requested that he drop them off at their hotel in Amsterdam. Before his friend could ask, the captain told him that the lives of Sonny and Vidya were in danger and it was important that they slipped away from the airport without being noticed; they would fill him in with the details during the drive to Amsterdam. "Okay, guys, jump into my jalopy," drawled the CIA station chief as he got into the driver's seat.

Sonny and Vidya crammed themselves into the car, and it drove off at 16:16 hours.

Using a shortcut, Li reached the immigration area at 16:17 hours and started his wait. He had calculated that the earliest his targets would arrive if they exited the aircraft early would be around 16:22 hours. He sat on a chair from where he could see everyone entering the immigration area and pretended to be dozing with earplugs in his ears; he was actually alert enough to notice a cockroach scoot by. The first passenger arrived around 16:22, just as Li had calculated, and the others followed in quick succession.

Li was all eyes, but there was no sign of Sonny and Vidya. At around 16:27 hours, as he started to wander, he noticed the captain, his co-pilot, and the crew walk in, but there was still no sign of either Sonny or Vidya. Li sensed that something was amiss; his face remained impassive as he walked up to the captain confidently and, introducing himself as an officer of the airport security, asked him about Sonny and Vidya as they were to be provided special security on government request.

'Oh them,' replied the captain, 'they left separately after the due immigration process, most probably for reasons of special security as alluded by you.' Li thanked him and walked away. His pace was measured, but his mind was racing: 'The aircraft landed at 16:00 hours, and the aero bridge was in place by 16:10 hours. The earliest they could have left would be after that and they were definitely headed to Amsterdam. He looked at his watch: it was 16:30 hour, so they had a head start of about twenty minutes.'

He called up the Deputy Chief of Mission (DCM) at the Chinese Embassy in Amsterdam, who was from the Chinese Internal Security Service, and with whom Li enjoyed a good rapport. Li informed the DCM that he was tracking two foreigners on Dan's instructions. He mentioned the likely movement of Sonny and Vidya to Amsterdam after 16:10 and asked the DCM to watch for them on the road from Schiphol Airport to Amsterdam.

As Li sent the photos of Sonny and Vidya on WeChat to the DCM, he also told him that they could have been assisted by the local station CIA Chief in their exit from the airport. Though the DCM was senior to Li for many years, and the Chinese Internal Security Service is hierarchical both by structure and ethos, he liked Li's professional commitment and ruthlessness, and the mention of Dan's name removed the remaining vestiges of reflexive hierarchical hostility.

He told Li that the speed cams placed on the highway would be able to provide the inputs he required and that his contact with the local traffic police was an efficient person. Li would hear from him shortly. Thanking him, Li made another call, this time to a Chinese hair stylist in Amsterdam, and fixed an appointment.

The Texan captain felt a surge of satisfaction as soon as Li inquired about Sonny and Vidya. It confirmed his suspicion that a reception party was indeed waiting for the duo, and that he had been denied landing at Eindhoven Airport for a reason—most likely a sinister one. Lost in his thoughts and with a smile on his lips, he came out of the airport, got into the taxi, and moved towards his hotel in Amsterdam.

After about 10 minutes, it occurred to him that he should inform Sonny about the Chinese coming up to him at the immigration and inquiring about them. He immediately dialled his friend, Station Chief CIA, and asked him to switch on his speakerphone so that all the occupants could listen in at the same time. He then told them about the Chinese, his question and confirmation that the denial of their landing request at Eindhoven was part of a diabolical plan to prevent Sonny and Vidya from carrying out their mission.

His friend asked him to describe the Chinese, and in reply, he said that the Chinese were wearing a sharp black suit with black brogue shoes. "Fair of skin with high cheekbones, the colour of his eyes and hair was black," the captain added. Vidya asked if there was anything else about him that the captain had noticed. "He appeared to be proficient in more than one language because after inquiring about you in English, he had taken out his mobile, called somebody and conversed in the Chinese language," the captain replied.

As the captain disconnected the call, the station chief drawled, "You guys sure are in trouble: this guy, in all probability, is a Chinese Internal Security Service agent who could be operating as a single-man hit squad or as part of a team tasked to abduct you."

"I suggest you guys lose yourself in the crowd quickly because the Chinese will come looking for you. Yes, take down my number and call me if you smell trouble." Mobile numbers were exchanged, and they were dropped off at Amsterdam Centraal, the city's bustling hub. Before he drove off, the station chief drawled, 'Remember, if things go south, head to the US Embassy.' Both nodded as the station chief waved with a broad grin and sped away.

Sonny and Vidya suddenly felt alone and looked at each other. Let's lose ourselves in the crowd, said Sonny, and as a first step, they decided to cancel their reservation at the Menninger Hotel and move to a cramped-up hostel near De Wallen, the red-light district of Amsterdam.

The hostel had double bunk accommodation with a common bathroom. They had put on their face masks during the journey from the airport to Amsterdam, but at the hostel, maintaining social distancing was nearly impossible. So, they decided to step out for a drink. The street was less crowded, the air was cool, and the flowing water in the canal was soothing. Sonny and Vidya sauntered through, soaking in the atmosphere, confident that they had eluded the Chinese agent; they entered a café for a glass of beer at 18:00 hours.

Love Li, sure that his prey would have moved to Amsterdam, drove straight to his hair stylist from the airport and reached the salon in half an hour.

As he was getting out of his car, his mobile rang. It was the DCM: he told Li that his contact was able to narrow down three cars, a challenging task as all the drivers and passengers were putting on masks and the pictures were grainy. He had all the cars followed, and one of them drove to Amsterdam Centraal. It was a Jaguar sports car, a model that was also driven by the CIA station chief.

Once the two passengers came out and bid goodbye to the driver, they could be identified with the help of the photographs: an American and an Indian, and the driver of the car, as per the inputs, was most probably the CIA station chief himself. "What time did they reach Amsterdam Centraal?" asked Li. "17:00 hours," replied the DCM, "but I kept tabs on them with the help of the CCTV cameras, and they moved into a hostel near De Wallen." Li requested the DCM to immediately place a surveillance team on the duo.

The DCM smiled into his mobile and confirmed that having anticipated this requirement, his team was already in place and would inform Li about the movements of the duo. Li's impassive face hardened a little in anticipation of the kill.

POISONOUS CHARM

He told his stylist to dress him with a silken blond hair wig which would give him a heart-aching, vulnerable look. Next, he put on some rouge on his cheeks, very light lipstick on his lips, a hint of kohl in his eyes and a pair of rimless round specs. He then changed into hip-hugging jeans and a tie with a powder blue jacket on top. Gone was the ruthless Chinese operative as Li transformed into a young and sensitive Dutch poet.

He came out of the saloon at 17:45 hours and started walking towards Amsterdam Centraal. At 18:00 hours, he got a call; Sonny and Vidya had entered a café in the area of De Wallen. Li changed direction, crossed the canal, and reached the bar at 18:10 hours. Once inside, he stood next to the entrance for a while to adjust his eyes to the dim lights and also locate his prey.

Sonny and Vidya had ordered a beer. Sonny was keen to sit at the bar counter and chat with the youngsters, but Vidya, not wanting to be noticed, opted for a corner table. Both ordered Heineken beer, gulped down their pints like thirsty crows, and ordered another round. They were sipping their second can when Li spotted them.

He went to the bar, picked up a pint of beer, and moved towards the duo. As he approached, Li made eye contact with Sonny, whose heart fluttered as he involuntarily smiled back. Li quickly looked away and sat at the next table, as though waiting for someone. Vidya, sitting opposite Sonny, hadn't noticed Li at first, but soon realized something was off as Sonny kept glancing furtively in his direction. To distract him, Vidya pointed to the painting of tulips and a windmill on the wall, casting a brief glance at Li. His glance showed him a slim young Dutch male in a slouch with a hint of femininity. His sixth sense told him that the Dutch spelt trouble.

He asked Sonny the reason for his fidgetiness and his barely concealed attempts to make eye contact with Dutch. Sonny replied, "I am not fidgety but am trying to establish contact and befriend the Dutch. If you remember, four of us had discussed Amsterdam as the melting pot of Europe because of weed and women, especially for those operating on both sides of the law and how that could be useful to us. I have a feeling that this guy will be of use to us."

As he completed the sentence, Sonny pushed back his chair and walked up to Li, who looked up, smiled, and asked him to sit down. Vidya watched Sonny as he walked up to Li, as if in a trance, and suddenly, it struck him; Sonny had fallen head over heels for the Dutch. His mind raced. The Dutch had entered after them and chosen to sit at the next table.

He appeared to be waiting for somebody, but no one had joined him until then. Was it just a coincidence, or was he fronting for the Chinese, luring them into a trap?

Vidya decided not to take any chances and joined Sonny and Li at their table. They were both in an animated conversation, their fingertips touching. Li had introduced himself as a poet with a fascination for the night, flowing water, the moon, and male love. He asked Sonny if he knew about the Afghan poems on male love. Sonny just smiled back, star-struck; Vidya felt totally left out of the conversation but was alert to the situation building up.

Li noticed their beer mugs were nearly empty and insisted on buying them a round of beer. They picked up their mugs and walked to the counter. Li requested the bartender to top them up. As the bartender was pouring the beer, Li felt the chunky sports watch on his right hand to reassure himself: the inside of the watch strap contained two mini glass vials filled with poison. Li had decided to mix poison in the duo's beer. The poison would take about half an hour to be effective; by then, Li would be out of Amsterdam driving back home.

His plan was working out smoothly as the American had fallen for him at first sight. They were all sipping beers together, and the conversation was warming up. Li decided to administer the poison in the third round of beers by pressing it out of the vials into their beer. By then, they would not be able to discern the slightly bitter taste of the poison.

Sonny was totally taken in by the Dutch poet, and his eyes were shining in admiration, while Vidya was more circumspect.

He had noticed the wristwatch on the right hand of the Dutch poet, which he found odd: most men wore their watches on the left hand. Unless the Dutch were playing a girl, he thought, because ladies normally wore their watches on the right hand. And if that was so, why was he wearing such a big and chunky sports watch? It should have been a more feminine wristwatch.

The events of the last three hours flashed back in Vidya's mind. Their pilot had requested a landing at

Eindhoven Airport, which was refused. A self-appointed reception team in the form of solo Chinese was lying in wait for them at Schiphol Airport. Now, this Dutch poet, who had walked into the bar after them and enticed Sonny, was having a beer with them. As Vidya's mind raced, Li cracked a joke, laughed, and threw back his head. Sonny laughed, too, and Vidya, who was lost in his thoughts, looked up. As he looked up, he thought he saw the slightest lift of the Dutch's blond hair, revealing a glimpse of black beneath it before Li quickly patted it back into place.

Vidya excused himself and moved towards the restroom. He had earlier noticed a Chinese waiter whom he signalled to. The Chinese waiter walked up to him and asked if he could be of help.

Vidya explained to him that he and his friends were meeting after a long time. Sonny, the American, claims that he has picked up the Chinese language well enough to understand and speak, and Vidya wanted to confirm it before laying a bet. He requested the Chinese waiter to come up within a yard of them and, with his back towards them, just call out 'listen' in Chinese in a slightly louder than normal tone. The Chinese waiter smiled and said that it was a nice way to find out before laying a bet: if Sonny reacted, the bets were off, and if he didn't, Vidya would be richer. The Chinese waiter was game but asked what was in it for him.

Vidya pressed a ten-dollar note into the waiter's hand and asked him to call out only after he returned to his seat. Back at the bar, Li had ordered another round of beer in a fresh set of beer mugs. The bartender placed two freshly filled beer mugs in front of Li. Rising from his bar stool, Li picked them up and walked over to Sonny, setting both mugs down in front of him. As he did, he locked eyes with Sonny and unable to resist, Sonny gently touched Li's face, as if brushing away a speck. Li smiled and pressed the vials into the two mugs. Sonny didn't notice a thing, but as Vidya returned to his seat, he saw the Dutch adjusting his watch strap over the two beers.

Sonny was all excited and told Vidya that the Dutch had got them another round of beer. 'Great,' replied Vidya, as he noticed the Chinese waiter and heard him utter a word. On hearing that word, the Dutch's head moved reflexively to follow the voice, but professional training prevented it from moving further and looking in the direction of the Chinese waiter.

A couple of seconds later, the Dutch turned around casually to locate the source of the sound, but the Chinese waiter was away, serving a table in the opposite corner. All this while, Vidya was totally focused on the Dutch, and the moment the Dutch's head moved ever so slightly to spot the source of the sound, Vidya's lips rounded, and he started whistling at a low pitch. All the dots, however faint, he had been able to connect it was clear that the Dutch was their unwelcome Chinese host in disguise, and something really harmful was cooking for them. Hearing Vidya whistle, the Dutch looked askance at him, and Sonny was visibly embarrassed. Vidya stopped whistling and offered his apologies, saying that it was an old, unwelcome habit that surfaced at the most inopportune time.

"All right, guys," called out Sonny, trying to get over the embarrassment, "let's do a bottom-up with our beer and then sip from the ones so benevolently offered by our Dutch friend." Vidya, who had noticed the Dutch adjusting his watch strap, immediately seconded Sonny's suggestion but said that it would be better done at the bar. Before Sonny could say anything, Vidya picked up the two poisoned beer glasses and, asking Sonny to bring his unfinished beer too, moved to the bar. Sonny and the Dutch, who were a little irritated by Vidya, followed suit. As Vidya reached the bar, he quickly exchanged the poisoned beer mugs with fresh ones, winked at the bartender, and pushed a ten-dollar bill across. The Dutch proposed a toast to their chance meeting and a budding friendship. They raised their beers and took a sip.

A couple of minutes earlier, the bartender had served the poison-laced beer to a young couple: a Nordic guy and a beautiful Georgian girl. They had walked in together and moved straight to the counter. Again, Vidya's watchful eyes noticed it.

The atmosphere in the café was warming up. Weed and cigarette smoke had begun to thicken and hang like a cloud.

Li had already planned his getaway: he would slink away immediately after the duo suffered a poison-induced massive heart attack and slumped into their respective chairs. By the time they would be noticed and found dead, he would have crossed the canal, walked to his car, taken off his disguise, and would be on his way to Vienna.

Meanwhile, Vidya brain texted Sonny that the Dutch were actually the Chinese in disguise who had inquired about them at the airport and had messed with their beers. He told Sonny that they needed to get away from the Chinese as soon as possible and asked him to go to the washroom, and said he would follow suit. Though taken aback, Sonny was sceptical about Vidya's input. But before he could protest, Husn texted that she knew the Chinese well, and they would do well to put maximum distance between them and the Chinese masquerading as a Dutch poet unless they were keen on an early and ruthless end to their young lives. The terse message from Husn hit its mark, and Sonny was shaken out of his fascination for the Dutch.

He excused himself and moved to the washroom, and Vidya followed suit. Li waited for them patiently, secure in the knowledge that Sonny had fallen for him hook, line, and sinker. Suddenly, there was a commotion at the bar.

Li looked up and saw the Nordic-Georgian couple slumped on the bar counter. He immediately sensed that something was amiss. He moved to the bar and, seeing the two unconscious bodies, realised that he had been outsmarted: the poison-laced beers meant for his prey had somehow been served to the unfortunate couple. He looked back at their table: it was empty.

He grimaced as he thought that he should have shot them with his silencer pistol as they sat drinking beer. Controlling his frustration and anger, he forced himself to think and plan on getting his prey soon.

Even before looking at the table, he knew that they would have left, and, in a split second, decided to waylay them in the dark lane just short of the hostel they had checked into. These guys were amateurs, so most likely, they would return to the hostel to pick up their stuff before scooting, Li thought. As he moved like a cheetah, fast & graceful, he called up the DCM and requested him to track them and provide their locations ASAP. DCM replied in a monosyllable, which sounded okay in Chinese, and hung up. Li took a shortcut which would get him, he calculated, into the ambush site at least five minutes before the unsuspecting duo walked into it. "They have made me run around so much, I will break their necks with my bare hands," mused Li as he moved.

Sonny was very cross with himself: "How could I be so stupid?" he thought to himself as he trooped behind Vidya.

They had taken but a moment in the washroom to decide to return to the hostel to pick up their stuff and relocate to another, safer place. Without a second thought, they had eased themselves out of the café and started running back to the hostel because they had foreseen that the Chinese, realising that he had been outsmarted the second time, would come after them sooner than later.

As they walked towards the hostel, Vidya sensed Sonny's despondency and texted him not to feel guilty but to use his brain to get them out of the present precarious situation. Vidya's message hit its mark, and Sonny, gaining confidence, tapped Vidya's shoulder and told him not to return to the hostel because the Chinese, having tracked them down to the café, would know about the hostel and most likely would be lying in wait for them. Vidya agreed, and they decided to move towards the Centraal. As they both moved swiftly, trying to keep in the shadows, Sonny called the CIA station chief and gave him the whole story.

Having heard Sonny out, the Station Chief told Sonny that the Chinese masquerading as the Dutch poet was apparently a professional hitman either hired or working for a country or powerful organisation that wanted both of them dead.

As he was talking to Sonny, the Station Chief had their location tracked through their mobiles and asked them to keep moving in the same direction for 500 metres and get into the by-lane to their right and wait for him there. He asked them to stay in the shadows and make no more calls. Sonny and Vidya reached the by-lane in about five minutes and waited without making themselves conspicuous.

As the Station Chief got into his car, he switched on his GPS; it would take him 15 minutes to reach the duo.

Li had reached the ambush site, barely out of breath, and waited for his prey. He had concealed himself skillfully like a tiger waiting to spring on its kill; he knew that surprise was the key element in springing a successful ambush.

Immediately after Li's call, the DCM requested his cyber police contact to locate the duo's mobiles. Being off duty, the contact took a little longer and added an extra convenience fee before passing on the duo's location as they waited for the Station Chief in the by-lane. Moments later, the information reached Li, who plotted it on the map. He was twenty minutes away by car, but if he crossed the canal and ran the rest of the way, he could cut five minutes off the time. Without hesitation, he crossed the canal.

The station chief's car was ten minutes away from the Rendezvous. Sony and Vidya waited anxiously for about 10 minutes in the by-lane before a black Jaguar sports car rolled by and stopped: the CIA station chief was on its wheel. He stopped the car, jumped out of it, uttered a muffled greeting and told them to take out the sims of their mobiles and crush them with their boots.

For a moment, both Sonny and Vidya appeared perplexed at the unusual request, looked quizzically at him, and then smiled as they realised that their mobiles, minus the sims, would emit no signal and the Chinese would lose their digital scent.

CIA Station chief told them that they had not a moment to lose as the Chinese would be closing in rapidly and asked them to hop into his car. The car had stopped at the by-lane for precisely two minutes before it took off for one of the safe houses within the US Embassy.

Li reached the spot five minutes later and found it deserted. He rang up the DCM to check the location of the duo. The DCM informed him that the duo's mobiles were at the same location until about five minutes ago, and then, all of a sudden, their digital signatures were lost. Love Li realised that they had again escaped from his clutches. They must have switched off their mobiles or, better still for them, would have taken the sims out of their mobiles, he thought.

Li was not used to such failures; he had eliminated all his quarries as planned. However, the Sonny–Vidya duo was proving to be a different kettle of fish. Li was beside himself with anger: the two greenhorns had given him the slip once again. He paused for a moment, closed his eyes, shut out all his thoughts, and meditated for a couple of minutes. It was enough for him to regain his equipoise and focus on the unfinished business; he had been outsmarted at the Schiphol Airport, outwitted at the bar, and outthought when he laid an ambush near the hostel. Li's mind, sharp as it was, told him that the duo were most likely high IQ guys who, in addition to being helped by the CIA, appeared to be situationally very aware. His face broke into a crooked smile as he realised that the duo was not just deer frozen in the headlights but slippery as eel; the challenge of the hunt, which brought the crooked smile on Li's face, also made his eyes gleam in anticipation. He decided to make two calls: first, he rang up the DCM and told him that when he reached the by-lane, he found it empty. Before he could say anything more, the DCM butted in to say that the duo's digital signatures had been lost about seven minutes ago, and he had fallen back on the CCTV cameras installed in the area. Sensing Li's impatience, the DCM quickly added that while the duo couldn't be spotted, a car had rolled into the by-lane and drove out after a couple of minutes. Zooming in on the car had given out more details.

It was the same Jaguar sports model which had picked them up from the airside of the airport. While grainy images weren't helpful in identifying the personal identities, two passengers cramped-up in the co-driver seat had been confirmed, and the car was moving at high speed towards the US Embassy. Li interjected and asked about the current location of the car: he was told that it was about five minutes away from the main entrance to the US Embassy.

As he listened, Li was calculating he would not be able to hit them before they entered the US Embassy as he was 20 minutes away from it, and extremely aggressive driving could only reduce the time to fifteen minutes; the duo, by then would not only be safely inside the embassy but most likely be inside one of the safe houses. Once they were inside the embassy, thought Li, eliminating the duo would be much more complex and could become a diplomatic hot potato. It may be more prudent to hit them once they were out of the Embassy, he reasoned with himself, but his mind countered, 'What if they did not come out of the embassy at all and were ferried out in a helicopter to the airport and from thereon in a special aircraft back to the USA.'

He decided to make the second call: it was to Dan. Dan picked up on the second ring and said, "Li, it has been more than four hours since the duo landed at Schiphol Airport. I hope you have rung up to give me the good news." Li gave him a rundown on what had happened till now and sought his go-ahead to eliminate them in the US Embassy itself. Dan started seething in anger when he heard Li's reply. His immediate reaction was to holler at Li, tell him that he was good for nothing, had let him down, and how the president would tear him, Dan, apart on hearing of the duo's escape into the safe sanctuary of the US Embassy, but he controlled himself. As a veteran of the shadowy world of spies and espionage, he also knew that Li was an invaluable asset, a racehorse which needed an expert rider to get the best out of him. Hitting the duo inside the US Embassy, he thought, was possible but would raise too many eyebrows. Aloud, he replied to Li, saying that he was deeply disappointed and that he, Love Li, should have catered to all the contingencies. Regarding granting permission to carry out the hit inside the US Embassy, he told Li that he would revert in 10 minutes.

Dawn had broken over Beijing as Dan glanced at his watch. It showed 06:30 hours local time.

Knowing that the president was an early riser, Dan dialled the presidential exchange and requested to speak to the president. Five minutes later, his phone rang. It was the presidential exchange, and he was put through to the president. Dan almost leapt out of his chair, stood at attention, and bowed ever so slightly as he wished the president good morning and followed it with a litany of fawning, informal, feel-good titles which only those very close to the president could utter. "Good Morning, Dan," replied the president as he smiled into his handset, secretly pleased by what he heard. Aloud, he said, "Give me some good news, Dan." As Dan made out that the president sounded fresh and cheery with no signs of a hangover, he thanked his stars; he knew that if the president nursed a hangover, he could be devastating in his manner.

Taking a deep breath, Dan gave a brief update on Love Li's mission and sought the president's permission to carry out the 'Hit' inside the US Embassy in Amsterdam. He also confirmed to the president that Love Li was capable of it.

Expecting the worst, Dan braced himself as he involuntarily moved the handset a little further away from his ear. He needn't have worried; displaying a clarity of mind possessed by only a few, the president's reply was both clear and precise.

"Do not carry out the operation while they are in the US Embassy, Dan," said the president, "hit them when they move out to visit the San Siro Stadium and leave no clues behind." Dan replied, "Yes, Sir, but what if the duo flew out of the embassy and on to the United States?" The president sounded indulgent as he asked Dan to do as he had been told before he hung up.

Dan realised that the president had been kind to him, but he also knew that he hated failures and could be ruthless in dealing with them.

He repeated the president's instructions verbatim to Li, whom he called up on WeChat immediately after his conversation with the president. When Li mentioned the contingency of the duo flying to the airport from the embassy and out of the country from there, Dan told him that the duo had been tasked to investigate Game Zero and would definitely visit the San Siro Stadium. And Li should plan on hitting them en route, while at the stadium, or on their return. Reminding Li not to leave any clues, Dan cut the call. Li wasn't entirely convinced by Dan's reasoning but was happy with the clear-cut instructions.

Li decided to contact an asset working at the US Embassy, informing him that two foreigners—an American named Sonny and an Indian named Vidya—had been escorted into the embassy earlier that day. He instructed the asset to monitor their movements and report their movements out of the embassy.

His asset told him that he would reach the embassy at 07:30 hours in the morning and call Li after locating the duo: the inputs from the CCTV camera footage, which he would get from friends in the embassy surveillance and operations centre, would come in most handy. The asset also told Li that he would be able to pick up their movement out of the embassy in real time and pass it to Li.

The next call Li made was to the DCM and shared with him the details of the planned 'Hit'; to the DCM, Li sounded a little worried and tired.

He suggested that Li drop in at his place and use the attic to knock off for a couple of hours: they could then discuss the plan in detail over a breakfast of soy milk and dumplings. Li replied in the affirmative, disconnected the phone, and turned his car towards the DCM's house.

Sonny was concerned about their belongings, especially their laptops, back at the hostel. So, the moment the station chief paused after confirming that they were moving to a safe house in the US Embassy, he told him that their belongings, including laptops, needed to be collected from the hostel. The station chief nodded and passed instructions for their collection to his embassy staff.

As they were being checked at the embassy entry gate, he got a call. It was the receptionist at the hostel wanting to confirm whether their stuff could be handed over to the embassy staff. Sonny took the mobile from the station chief and spoke with her: all their stuff was handed over as instructed.

At the entry gate, the station chief filled in all the details about Sonny and Vidya, signed a few documents and escorted them to a safe house.

He left a message for the ambassador about both of them, which would be seen in the morning by him.

It was midnight as they entered the safe house, and the station chief told them to get some rest. He said that he would meet them after breakfast, which would be served at 07:30 hours. As he turned to leave, Sonny requested that he provide the recording of Game Zero, specifically of the CCTV cameras covering all the entries, exits, parking areas, and stadium, including the team locker rooms and the members' enclosure. The station chief suppressed a yawn and said, "Okay, Sonny, will do, but it's time for both of you to hit the sack."

Sonny, apparently, was not done as yet. He was bright as light with his focus on Game Zero at the San Siro Stadium: he requested the station chief to sit with them for 10 minutes and help work out a plan for the next days. The station chief smiled and said, "Sorry, Sonny, we need to sleep over it." As he walked off, Vidya, grinning, told Sonny that parts of the human brain continue to be active while the person is asleep and that solutions are provided during sleep also!

Five minutes after the station chief walked out of the safe house, the duo's belongings, collected from the hostel, were delivered to them.

At 07:30 hours the next day, as Li walked down from the attic to join the DCM for soy milk and dumplings, the US station chief guffawed his way into the safe house where Sonny and Vidya were waiting for him.

Li sat down on the chair opposite the DCM and came straight to the point. He told the DCM that he had been categorically instructed not to carry out the hit inside the embassy so he could do it from the time they stepped out of the embassy to the time they re-entered it. He further elaborated that in all probability, the duo, as per inputs, would visit the San Siro Stadium, which meant that they could be hit as they moved to the stadium, while they moved around in it and on their return to the embassy. He also confirmed that he had an asset inside the embassy who would pass on the location and movement details of the duo to him in real-time.

DCM took a sip of soya milk and told Li that the hit could be carried out anytime between their stepping out of the embassy and up to their return the embassy, provided they returned because they could decide to move from the San Siro Stadium directly to the airport or by road to any of the neighbouring countries. So, he opined that the hit should be carried out when the duo is moving to the San Siro Stadium or within the stadium itself.

Li nodded in agreement and added that Dan had told him not to leave any clues behind, so it would be better if the hit was carried out in a clean and quiet manner with no collateral damage.

DCM thought for a while and then said, "Li, if you want a sure-shot way without leaving behind any clues, go in for a sniper hit, and the right place would be the San Siro Stadium." Li was happy with DCM's suggestion and asked for help with getting him a Barrett M82 sniper rifle. Li was a staunch nationalist, but he also was a trained sniper and knew which was the best sniper rifle in the world!

DCM knew that he was not obliged to help Li as he was on a lone wolf mission, but he liked Li for his remorse-free killing proficiency, and he knew that Li would definitely share details of the help provided by the DCM for the operation with Dan. Aloud, he said that he would arrange for the sniper rifle with ammunition from Brussels through an ex-Belgian special operative who was now an arms dealer.

As Li sat quietly, the DCM rang up his contact and requested that he supply the sniper rifle as soon as possible. His contact, a man of few words, quoted him a price which was unrealistically high. He covered the mouthpiece and told Li the price. Li nodded yes but whispered that the amount would be wired on receipt of the weapon, which should be made soonest. The DCM repeated Li's sentence verbatim, and the person on the other side said only one word, 'done', and cut the call. A few seconds later, DCM received a message confirming delivery by lunchtime. He looked up at Li and smiled.

The CIA station chief was trying to convince Sonny and Vidya to give San Siro Stadium a go-by and return to the US immediately. He told them that they were up against professional killers and did not stand a chance against them. Sonny, who was doing most of the talking, argued that they had been sent on a mission ordered by the POTUS himself, and they could not return empty-handed. "Fine," said the station chief, "what I will then suggest is that you guys lie low for a few days because the Chinese hitman will, in all probability, be waiting for you outside. By now, he would know that you are holed up here, and I would not be surprised if he had some local embassy employee on his payroll who was constantly passing him information about you."

Sonny conveyed that they could ill afford to lie low for a few days because they had been given but a week's time to prepare the application. Vidya, who was quietly listening in, looked at Sonny and said that they had been given a week to develop the application, but it did not include finding out the origins of the virus and evidence of foul play, if any. He suggested that Sonny speak with POWAP and seek two additional weeks to develop the application and simultaneously investigate the origins and spread of the virus.

Sonny nodded and started typing an email for POWAP.

Vidya looked at the station chief and requested the CCTV recording of the day of Game Zero at the San Siro Stadium, starting from midnight through to Game Zero and an hour beyond it, including all roads leading to the San Siro Stadium from about four kilometres out. "It's all settled then," said the station chief, "both of you are going to cool your heels here for a few days and work on the application. In the meantime, I will work out a way for you to visit the San Siro Stadium and carry out your investigation without the Chinese being any wiser about your location or movement. I should also be able to get hold of the CCTV recording, as requested, today itself and send it across." As he got up to go, he added that all meals would be served to them inside the safe house and advised them not to come out, even on the patio, to avoid detection.

Unknown to them, Li's asset inside the embassy had already traced their entry into the embassy from the reception log. He also knew that they would be in one of the two safe houses within the embassy premises.

After the station chief left, Sonny and Vidya decided to do the dishes and then have a cup of coffee. As they were doing the dishes, Sonny told Vidya that he had two friends in Amsterdam, better known as 'Ice Lilies', who could be helpful in getting them to San Siro Stadium.

Vidya, lost in his thoughts and drowsy as well, just muttered, "We could use all the help that we could get, but it would be worth its while to check with POWAP." While they sipped their coffee, Sonny shot off an email to POWAP, who, knowing that POTUS was an early riser, forwarded it to him requesting a decision.

It was early morning in Washington, and POTUS replied within minutes, giving his permission to seek help from Sonny's friends, with a caveat that minimal information about their mission be shared with them.

Chapter 5

Changi and Starfish: Hurdles and Help

The aircraft carrying Husn and Aashiq was about half an hour away from Changi Airport, Singapore, and Husn was busy describing it in detail to Aashiq. Confirming that it had been rated as the world's best airport for the last eight years, Husn told him about its butterfly, orchid, and cactus gardens, the rooftop swimming pool, and the movie theatre. Keeping the best for the last, she told Aashiq about the five-storied forest and the highest indoor waterfall that had been created and become functional recently: christened as the Jewel, passengers could visit, relax, and trek up to the highest point of the waterfall through the five-storied forest, she added.

Aashiq was all agog with excitement and pleaded with Husn for a visit to the Jewel before taking off for Beijing. Husn nodded and called Kun Kar, who was in the middle of a meeting. He excused himself, moved out of the conference room, and rang her back. He realised his breathing had become quicker and shallower. The moment he heard Husn's voice, his stomach tightened.

Husn informed him that their aircraft was to land at the Changi Airport in half an hour and asked him if they could be conducted through the Jewel before taking off for Beijing. Kun Kar replied in the affirmative and added that she and Aashiq would be received at terminal 1 and, two hours later, a specially chartered flight would take off from terminal 4 for Beijing with both of them on board. So they would have enough time to visit the Jewel. As Husn thanked him, he told her that he was really looking forward to their meeting in Beijing. As he hung up, he reminded himself to arrange for caterpillar fungus, a Chinese aphrodisiac, before Husn's arrival.

Changi Airport was its usual bustling hub, filled with passengers, workers, and security staff. Among them were two sisters, Anne and Mary Lee, who fit into none of these categories; as members of the Big Circle Gang, they were there on a far more sinister and deadly mission.

Chinese Triad Society, the Big Circle Gang, was a century-old organisation which originated in Shanghai, a port city and a prosperous business hub.

Ma, a local businessman, and Dang, a local government officer, were friends. Ma resided in a palatial house, and a couple, Mong Li and his wife, Ming Li, worked as house servants for Ma. Dang would often be invited over by Ma to his house, where he would be served by Ming. Ming was a young and beautiful village belle who had accompanied Mong to Shanghai soon after he married her. His village was not far from Ming's, and both had studied together in primary school.

Dang was besotted by Ming's charms. He requested Ma to join him for a boat ride on his houseboat and bring Mong and Ming Li to help out with cooking and serving. Ma agreed and took Mong and Ming along with him to

Dang's houseboat on the weekend. The dinner was served on the deck. It was a full moon night, and the weather was very pleasant, with a gentle and cool breeze that kept the humidity away.

While retiring for the night, Dang told Ming to bring some drinking water for him in his cabin. After cleaning up the table and the deck, Ming went to Dang's cabin with drinking water. As she kept the water tumbler on the bedside table, Dang held her from behind and started kissing and groping her. Ming was caught unaware and shrieked. Dong had unusually big hands, and he put the left one on Ming's mouth to keep her from shouting, but it also covered her nose. For a couple of minutes, Ming struggled too hard to free herself and then suddenly slumped down to the ground.

Dang panicked, picked her up and threw her into the water. She actually died by drowning. Her body was found floating after three days. The story put out was that she slipped while returning from Dang's room, but her husband, Mong, knew the truth. He had seen Dang throw Ming into the water.

For Ma and Dang, it was business as usual after commiserating Ming's unfortunate death, but Mong was deeply disturbed and vowed to avenge his wife's murder. He knew that his word against Dang's would hold no water, and he, too, could face a very bleak future. Mong was a poor hillbilly, instinctively loyal to his master. He carried out his chores without any hint of distress, anger, or frustration. However, the rich miss out on the risk-taking ability of the poor because they have very little to lose anyway.

Mong requested some leave of absence and returned to his village. There, he went to Ming's family and told them the whole story. Ming was the eldest child, and she had two younger sisters and two younger brothers. The sisters were older , and the older of the two sisters was just a year younger than Ming. Her name was Su Li, and she looked quite like Ming herself.

After narrating the story to Ming's parents, Mong asked for Su's hand and promised them that he would avenge Ming's murder through Su.

The parents agreed, and Ming returned to Shanghai with Su as his new wife. Su knew what had happened to her sister, and she was as keen as Mong to avenge her murder. Mong told her that in due course, Dang would notice her and would not be able to resist her charms. He would again invite Ma to his boat along with Mong and Su because of the privacy it afforded him. Once on the boat, Dang would, in all probability, call her to his cabin after dinner on some errand and take advantage of her. Mang told Su not only to play along but also to encourage Dang subtly in a way that only a lady could do. Once in the cabin, Su would offer a glass of sedative-laced wine and dare him to gulp it down. The sedative would make Dang unconscious in five minutes, and after making sure that Dang was unconscious, Su would signal Mong, who would be waiting outside.

Mong's simple plan proved effective. Dang noticed Su the next time he came to Ma's place. He also noticed she looked quite similar to Ming but was bolder and gave him furtive glances. Initially, Dang steeled himself against falling for Su, reminding himself of Ming's unfortunate affair. But he couldn't resist for long as his mind told him that Su was herself interested in his manly charms. A month later, Dang invited Ma over to his boat along with Mong and Su and, after dinner, asked her to get water for him in his cabin.

Su reached his cabin with the water tumbler and kept it on his bedside table. Dang caught her wrist and pulled her toward him. She did not resist and melted in his arms. Dang pulled up her face and tried to plant a kiss on her lips. She slipped out of his grasp and said that they should have some wine to enjoy the night and slowly stoke the fire. Dang agreed readily and pointed her towards the bar. She took out two glasses and a bottle of wine from the cabinet and, turning her back towards Dang, laced his glass with poison before pouring wine; it was served to Dang on a tray.

Su kissed Dang lightly on his lips and suggested a 'bottoms up' to let the first drink burn through the throat into the stomach before sipping the second glass of wine in bed together. Saying, 'Ganbei', both of them gulped down their wine. Su refilled the empty glasses before Dang pulled her into the bed and started kissing her. Su played along, knowing what was to come. Dang suddenly slumped as he was trying to get on top of Su. She checked, found him well sedated, stepped out of the cabin and called Mong inside. Both of them picked up Dang's limp body and tossed it over the rails into the water; Dang, too, died by drowning!

Mong walked up to Ma and told him the whole story regarding the death of Ming and Dang.

Ma advised him to disappear into the backwaters of Shanghai, warning that the police would soon come looking for him. He cautioned against returning to his village, as the authorities would likely track him down there and arrest him.

Mong and Su immediately took off with their bundles of belongings and found a small room in the shanty town near the Shanghai harbour, which housed the daily wage labourers. Mong started working as a longshoreman, loading and unloading cargo from the ships, and Su started providing simple and cheap Chinese meals from a makeshift takeaway place. Mong kept in touch with Ma all along.

Six months later, Ma requested Mong to knock off a business associate who had fallen foul of Ma because of non-payment of dues and was scheming to have Ma killed. Ma also promised a tidy sum to Mong after the completion of the task.

Mong agreed to do Ma's bidding and returned to his shanty to discuss the 'how' of the task with Su. Both discussed in detail and finally decided on an encore of Dang's drowning: the bait would be Su, the knock-out punch would be poison, and the disposal of the body would be in the sea.

Ma provided them with a ten percent advance to cover the working costs, and it took the couple about three weeks to have their prey consigned to a watery grave.

Ma paid them the balance of the promised amount, and with the first successful contract killing, the Big Circle Gang started taking shape.

Initially, it was just Mong and Su. They purchased a one-bedroom pucca house. Mong became a stevedore, and Su started a small eatery. Slowly, the Big Circle Gang began expanding, taking in new members, mostly labourers or longshoremen from Mong's village. Contract killings started coming their way, and gradually, both the scope of the work and the number of members of the Big Circle Gang increased. Besides contract killings, a distribution network of opium and smuggling of other items was also taken on by the gang.

Its new members continued to be men and women from the villagers of the region. Within five years of its inception, the Big Circle Gang was a Triad society with a complete ecosystem. There was a well-established hierarchy, an allegiance of oath, and a code of conduct. Undying loyalty was the strong suit of the gang; each member and his/her family were taken care of, and women were given the pride of the place because they could lure easily and kill ruthlessly. Over a period of time, the gang spread its tentacles within China and abroad in places with sizeable Chinese populations. Its members were exclusively Chinese or of Chinese descent. The presence of Chinatowns in many countries around the world worked to their advantage.

The orders to eliminate Husn and Aashiq were issued from Shanghai to Singapore, where the head of the Big Circle Gang's Singapore branch summoned Anne and Mary Lee. The two sisters, aged 22 and 20, were born to Chinese parents settled in Singapore. Devout Christians, they worked as sales associates at an international clothing retailer. They were also members of the Big Circle Gang and possessed proven killer instincts and skills.

They were briefed by the head to carry out the hit in Changi Airport itself: he informed them that the targets would be moving from terminal 1 to terminal 4 to take a chartered flight to Beijing two hours after their arrival and advised that they were best taken out enroute and silently, leaving behind no clues.

Anne asked him if their programme for the two hours between their arrival and departure was known. The head replied in negative but added that, in all likelihood, he would be able to find out within minutes of their arrival and convey it to Anne. Anne and Mary Li were at the airport at terminal 1 an hour before the scheduled arrival of Husn and Aashiq. They were wearing the Sarong-Kebaya uniform worn by Singapore International Airlines air hostesses. They had smuggled themselves in a catering van, which was cursorily checked, and entered the basement of the terminal building from the airside.

They moved the food trolleys to the pantry utilising the service lift and then moved into a ladies' restroom to change into their air hostess uniform and moved out to terminal 1 to await their quarry.

They had opted to use cyanide-tipped miniature arrows, launched discreetly with a rubber band across the fingers. Silent, swift, and deadly, the weapon guaranteed a target's death within ninety seconds. This method was tried and tested for them, with six successful kills already attributed to the miniature cyanide arrows.

After Husn made her request, Kun Kar called up the Chinese military attaché and told him to make the necessary arrangements for the duo to visit the Jewel before their departure for Beijing. The military attaché, in turn, called up the Changi Airport CEO and requested him to make the necessary arrangements. Coming from the Chinese military attaché, the CEO acted with alacrity and put his protocol officer on the job. One minute before the aircraft carrying Husn and Aashiq touched down, the protocol officer reached terminal 1 to receive and conduct them through the Jewel.

As the CEO of Changi Airport briefed the protocol officer, his secretary, a petite Chinese Singaporean in her thirties, passed all the details to the Head of the Big Circle Gang, Singapore module, including the protocol officer's mobile number and photograph. The head called up Anne and gave her the details of the duo's programme and asked her to meet the protocol officer as he sent her his photograph.

His next call was to the protocol officer. After introducing himself, the head told him to cooperate with Anne and Mary if he wanted 10,000 US dollars and the safety of his family. Anne and Mary were by the protocol officer's side as he disconnected the call.

Without bothering to introduce themselves, Anne tersely instructed the protocol officer to bring the duo to the Jewel after 30 minutes and get them to stop for a minute or so in the area where the five-storied jungle was the thickest. The protocol officer blinked and then nodded affirmatively.

Husn and Aashiq were at the immigration as Anne spoke to the protocol officer. Within minutes, they were through the immigration. They noted that there were hardly any international travellers because of the pandemic. Right after the immigration, they were received by the protocol officer, who introduced himself and informed them that he would guide them to their flight from terminal 4 and would also conduct them through the newly inaugurated Jewel.

Husn and Aashiq were both jet-lagged after the long journey, but Jewel's mention perked them up. Husn, more at ease with the surroundings and people, told the protocol officer that they would be ready to see the Jewel after collecting their baggage, freshening up, and gulping down a cup of black and strong coffee at the Starbucks outlet.

The protocol officer, unfailingly polite, informed Husn that he would pick them up from the Starbucks location in thirty minutes.

Anne and Mary had reconnoitred the five-storied jungle in detail to select a spot which could afford them engagement of the targets from close range while providing enough foliage to conceal themselves fully. They had also carried with them camouflage army dungarees which they changed into as the protocol officer reached the Starbucks outlet and met Husn and Aashiq.

Within five minutes of their changing into camouflage dungarees, Anne and Mary were in their positions on the first storey of the jungle. They would shoot down their arrows onto their targets, which would be just 6 to 8 metres away, and they were well concealed. It was already decided between them that Anne would target Husn while Mary would take out Aashiq.

Anne had with her a pocket-sized slim binocular through which she spotted the protocol officer, Husn, and Aashiq walking towards the Jewel. Anne alerted Mary that the targets were about 500 metres away and they would be in their crosshairs in the next 5 to 7 minutes. Mary was sitting next to Anne on her haunches, and both of them appeared like bonsais in their camouflage dungarees. Both Anne and Mary checked their cyanide-tipped arrows and rubber bows and carried out a mock kill. Their targets were still three minutes away, and, to relieve the tension, Mary joked that she found Aashiq handsome enough to make love to before taking him out.

Anne smiled and relaxed, but as hard-boiled assassins, a minute before their quarry was to reach, their minds went blank as they focused on their task.

Husn and Aashiq had collected their baggage, freshened up in the lounge, and headed to the Starbucks outlet, where they ordered sandwiches and espresso coffee. Aashiq had not been able to get much sleep on the aircraft and joked that he could drop-dead at any moment because of jet lag. Husn told him to eat his sandwich and drink up the coffee, and he would feel much better. As they finished their coffee, the protocol officer walked up to their table and requested that they accompany him to the Jewel.

Both of them got up and moved with their wheelie bags in their right hands. Now that Husn had opened up to Aashiq and, in turn, Aashiq had confirmed that he would be her friend for life, she felt relaxed and, asking Aashiq to shift his bag to his left hand, took his right hand in her left and gave it a squeeze. Aashiq, pleasantly surprised, squeezed back, and hand in hand, they walked to the Jewel.

Anne noticed that their targets were walking abreast and whispered to Mary that they would release the arrows once their respective targets had crossed them, so that they would be hit on the back of their necks simultaneously. As the arrows would hit home, Anne and Mary would make a quick and silent exit, change into air hostess uniforms in the ladies' restroom, and take a taxi home..

Anne whispered to Mary that the targets were a minute away. Both of them carried out their last-minute checks and, thirty seconds later, pushed the cyanide-tipped miniature arrows across the bow framed between their forefinger and middle finger. Ten seconds before the release of the arrow, they would hold their breath, be steady like a rock, and breathe only after releasing the arrow.

Husn and Aashiq strolled slowly, hand in hand, marveling at the masterpiece created by the brilliant Singaporeans. The protocol officer was moving slightly ahead of them, explaining the concept of the Jewel. As they reached the spot, conveyed by Anne to the protocol officer, he stopped to explain about the five-storied forest. Husn and Aashiq, too, stopped, the rear of their necks clearly visible to Anne and Mary. Anne whispered, "Three, two, one," and both let their arrows fly. The moment the arrows were released, Husn and Aashiq became sitting ducks, as the cyanide-tipped projectiles would send them into eternal sleep within minutes. But as the saying goes, "Man proposes, and God disposes." Just as Anne fired her arrow, she watched in surprise as Aashiq collapsed, pulling Husn down with him.

Both the arrows which were to hit their respective targets sailed harmlessly into the forest area created on the opposite side. With both Aashiq and Husn collapsing to the ground, there was a sudden commotion as people rushed to help. The protocol officer, while requesting people not to crowd around, rang up the medical emergency and gave them his location. With typical Singaporean efficiency, the medical emergency team reached Aashiq within minutes of his collapse. Husn, in the meantime, had gotten up and got hold of herself. Realizing that jet lag, fatigue, and lack of proper food had likely caused Aashiq to collapse, she loosened his belt, untied his shoelaces, removed his shoes, and asked the protocol officer for some water.

Three minutes after he had collapsed, Aashiq opened his eyes and gave a weak smile. He felt wasted and groggy. Husn got him to drink some water from a water bottle. With help, Aashiq got up and, holding on to Husn, walked to the nearby sitting area. The medical emergency team checked his vital parameters and found them normal. He was afebrile, did not have a cough or cold, and a quick antigen test confirmed that he was COVID-19 negative.

Finally, the doctor, a jovial, portly Singaporean of South Indian descent boasting a pearl-white set of teeth and dark mahogany skin, ruled that Aashiq needed rest and energy. It was decided to move him on the electric buggy to the chartered aircraft and administer a saline drip. He also gave Husn a tablet of Alprax and asked her to get Aashiq to take it after he had eaten something. It would help him get some sleep and rest," the doctor told Husn.

Both sisters, after firing the arrows, moved out of the forest area immediately. They knew better than to try to hit their targets again with cyanide-tipped arrows with so much commotion and people around. Once inside the nearby restroom, Anne called up the head and gave him all the details of how the arrows missed the targets. She added that if permitted, they would get the duo before they boarded the aircraft. She did not know that the duo had been moved to the aircraft already. She was told to be in the restroom and await further orders. He, in turn, called up Shanghai and offered another go at the duo.

He was told that the duo had already been moved into the aircraft, so another attempt was possible only in the aircraft. Unknown to the Singapore cell, the protocol officer had been contacted by Shanghai and instructed to keep them updated with the latest. He was passing cryptic messages to them on WeChat. Therefore, Shanghai already knew of the missed assassination attempt, Aashiq blacking out, and being moved straight to the aircraft for treatment.

The Singapore Head of the Big Circle Gang cell was told to get Anne and Mary on board the chartered aircraft as air hostesses and poison the duo just before landing so that Anne and Mary had adequate time to move to a safe house in Beijing and from there to Shanghai. The instructions were very specific about the poison; it was to take effect only after two hours of its administration.

Anne and Mary were still in the ladies' restroom when they got the call instructing them to change into their air hostess uniforms and board the chartered aircraft scheduled to take off in an hour from terminal four. Husn and Aashiq were to be poisoned half an hour before the flight was scheduled to land in Beijing.

The poison would be delivered to them in a special package before the aircraft took off for Beijing. Instructions had already been passed to the airport and immigration authorities to enlist them on bonafide duty. They were also given instructions regarding their movements after landing at the Beijing airport. Unknown to them, the poison had already been procured, and a motorcycle-borne rider was on his way to terminal four of Changi Airport. The poison package would be delivered to Anne thirty minutes before the scheduled take-off of the chartered aircraft.

Anne and Mary quickly changed out of their sweaty camouflage dungarees, applied perfume, and then took an electric buggy to Terminal 4. They boarded the aircraft just 15 minutes before its scheduled takeoff time. Aashiq and Husn had already boarded the aircraft. Aashiq was settled in and administered saline on a seat that had been converted into a bed. He had already finished a large bowl of chicken soup and taken the Alprax tablet Husn had given him, leaving him feeling drowsy.

He would be asleep before the take-off and would awake only half an hour before their arrival in Beijing. A medical attendant had helped Husn administer the saline, while a caring, matronly air hostess tended to all the other needs of both Aashiq and Husn. Husn quickly took a liking to her, and before long, the two were chatting as if they were old friends reconnecting after years.

Ten minutes later, Husn noticed two young air hostesses in Singapore Airlines uniform, and she thought that they were being treated like VIPs with so many air hostesses to look after just the two of them. She wondered if Kun Kar was behind it all. Husn looked at

Aashiq; he was fast asleep, and she, too, decided to make herself comfortable and get some sleep. She was about to press the air hostess sign when she saw the matronly air hostess walking up to her along with the two younger Singapore Airlines air hostesses, whom she introduced as Mai Li and Sai Li. She said that between the two, they would take care of all Husn's needs.

Husn smiled at Mai Li and Sai Li and requested them to help her convert her seat into a comfortable bed. The matronly air hostess left quickly without a word. After she was tucked into her bed, Husn requested Mai Li to send the matronly air hostess to her.

Husn had noticed that the matronly air hostess was not herself when she introduced Mai Li and Sai Li.

A couple of minutes later, the matronly air hostess was by her side and, on asking, replied that she had been told to let Mai Li and Sai Li look after the two guests. Husn was not convinced and asked her why she was so subdued. The matronly air hostess stared at her blankly and then whispered that Husn should examine the inside of Mai Li and Sai Li's right wrists.

Husn asked loudly for a Diet Coke, which Sai Li brought to her. As she took the paper cup from Sai Li, Husn complimented her on her pretty hands and, gently holding Sai Li's right hand, caressed it affectionately.

While doing so, Husn was looking deep into Sai Li's eyes, and she suddenly looked over her shoulder. Sai Li involuntarily followed Husn's gaze towards the cockpit, giving Husn enough time to glance at her wrist.

Husn's eyes registered a miniature tattoo of a Chinese symbol denoting a circle. She released Sai Li's hand, thanked her once again, and took a sip of Diet Coke. Her head was reeling. She had immediately connected the dots with regard to the matronly air hostess's behaviour, her hint, and the tattoo on Sai Li's wrist. Husn knew about the Big Circle Gang, its reach, and lethality.

If Mai Li and Sai Li were members of the Big Circle Gang, Husn thought, their presence on the aircraft spelt trouble. They, Husn and Aashiq, could be the only targets because the rest were all crew members. She knew she had not a moment to lose as the aircraft was to take off in the next five minutes. She called Kun Kar Li on WeChat and prayed that he would pick up.

Kun Kar Li was attending a high-stakes Politburo meeting. His phone was on silent, tucked in his left pocket. When he felt a slight vibration, his first instinct was to ignore it, but then he reconsidered— it could be important. He discreetly pulled out the phone and saw Husn's name. He knew excusing himself to take the call would be seen as bad form, especially in such a critical meeting. After all, this was the most powerful committee in China, and even though the president was his friend, he could be very sensitive to any perceived slight.

So, KunKar disconnected the call and messaged, asking her to message on WeChat. It was three minutes to take off, and Husn knew that she would lose connectivity a couple of minutes after take-off because the signal strength weakened as the aircraft gained height in this part of the world. It was one minute to take off when KunKar received her message. The moment he read about the two air hostesses with circle tattoos on their wrists, he realised that the Big Circle Gang had been contracted to bump off Husn and Aashiq. Husn received his reply a minute after take-off, telling her not to worry but to remain alert to any action from the two air hostesses.

Kun Kar, knowing the lethality and effectiveness of the Big Circle Gang, caught the president's attention and, through his eyes, conveyed that he had an important and urgent input. The president quickly announced that he needed a brief break, and the meeting was adjourned for ten minutes. Seizing the opportunity, Kun Kar followed the president to the restroom to speak with him.

The president's personal bodyguard gave Kun Kar a questioning look, as it was customary for no one to use the restroom while the president was inside. Kun Kar waved dismissively, reassuring the guard, and then, standing beside the president, quickly explained the situation in the aircraft.

The president received the message calmly and told Kun Kar that Husn and Aashiq were coming to Beijing and visiting the WVI to carry out an investigation for them, which was both important and sensitive. Later, after the investigation had been carried out successfully, the Big Circle Gang could knock them off, but for now, they had to lay off or else face disastrous consequences. As the president washed his hands at the sink, he asked Kun Kar to call Dan and asked him to ensure the safety of Husn and Aashiq until their visit and investigation at WVI were successful.

A minute later, Kun Kar relayed the president's instructions to Dan, stressing that the duo should not be harmed until they had finished their investigation and submitted their report. Only after receiving the president's approval could any action be taken against them. Dan listened carefully and, once Kun Kar had finished, immediately confirmed that the Big Circle Gang would follow the president's orders without question.

The politburo meeting reconvened after the break, but Dan's chair, as he was a special invitee to the meeting to discuss the current situation on the border with India, was empty. He was already on his way to Beijing airport and had told his driver to press on the accelerator.

Realising the gravity of the situation, he had already called his deputy, Deng and instructed him to contact Hong, the leader of the Big Circle Gang. He asked Deng to arrange for Hong to meet him at the ATC of Beijing airport in 20 minutes. True to his loyal nature, Deng was already at the airport with Hong when Dan arrived at Beijing Daxing International Airport, and the three of them headed to the ATC.

The chartered flight carrying Husn and Aashiq was airborne 45 minutes ago, and it was cruising at a height of 29,000 feet at slightly below Mach speed.

Aashiq was fast asleep, and Husn was fully awake. After she had received KunKar's message to be alert, she reconverted her bed back into an armchair and asked Mai Li to send the matronly air hostess to her. The matronly air hostess came to Husn, her face tired and drawn, and asked what she could do for Husn.

Husn told her that some help might be on its way and that until then, she should sit in the crew seat next to the cockpit and keep an eye on the rear of the aircraft where Mai Li and Sai Li were sitting. Husn also requested her to give a signal in case either Mai Li or Sai Li or both moved up towards the front of the aircraft. The matronly air hostess nodded and took up her position as instructed.

Husn was wide awake and fully alert; she was taking no chances with the Big Circle Gang and had decided not to go down without a fight. She also decided to shake Aashiq awake and warn him in case she sensed danger.

Husn was finding it difficult to be awake and alert because of the jet lag and the eventful brief stopover at the Changi Airport. As she appeared to doze off, she noticed the matronly air hostess stiffening while looking towards the rear of the aircraft. In a flash, Husn took out her pocket-sized vanity mirror and, through it, saw both Mai Li and Sai Li walking towards her. She snapped open her safety belt, got up, and tapped Aashiq awake.

Aashiq opened his eyes and groggily inquired whether they had taken off for Beijing or not. Husn replied in the affirmative and told him to be alert. By now, Mai Li and Sai Li were almost abreast, and Husn turned outward to face them, shielding Aashiq with her body. Both the Li sisters smiled at her as they crossed her and continued towards the cockpit.

As they rode up in the lift, Dan conveyed the president's message to Hong, who listened. For him, it was just another contract hit, and the request was for its postponement, not cancellation. Hong, who prided himself as the king rat, understood the power of the president well. He confirmed to Dan that no harm would come to Husn and Aashiq until a go-ahead was received. In about two and a half minutes, they reached the ATC, which was a sprawling hall with four rows of thirty screens, each being manned by a controller.

Dan briefly introduced Deng and Hong to the Director and told him that an urgent message needed to be passed to the chartered aircraft, which was to land in another four hours at 'Starfish'. He followed up by saying that the message was for the two Singapore Airlines air hostesses travelling in the aircraft, and it was for their ears only.

For the director, it was an unusual request, but he knew about Dan and also that the government's request could not be trifled with: he nodded and asked them to follow him as he led them to the controller, who was in touch with the chartered aircraft.

As they moved to the controller, Dan told the director that Hong would be passing the message and that nobody else should be in the vicinity as it involved the highest level of national security. The director, a thoroughbred professional, barely acknowledged Dan's message before contacting the aircraft and asking the captain to get the air hostesses in the cockpit. Once the captain confirmed their arrival, he asked all controllers in the near vicinity to leave and also told the captain and his co-pilot to step aside and not listen to the communication about to take place.

After the director walked away, Hong bent over the speaker and, introducing himself in Chinese, instructed them to defer all plans until they landed in Beijing, where they would receive fresh instructions.

Li sisters were taken aback for a moment but had heard about Hong and well understood that his message had to be obeyed without any doubt. Anne confirmed the same to Hong and both of them walked back to the aircraft.

The captain and co-pilot were back in their seats, as was their ATC controller, while the director escorted the trio back to the lift. Thanking the director, they got into the lift, got off on the ground floor and, after a quick shake of hands, got into their cars and drove off.

Once inside his car, Dan heaved a sigh of relief; he was able to avert a catastrophe in the nick of time without any hiccups.

Dan called up the president through the exchange and confirmed to him that Husn and Aashiq would not be harmed by the Big Circle Gang until a go-ahead was given to them. The president grunted and told Dan to keep a close watch because the Big Circle Gang was, after all, a detestable grouping of killers, thugs, and drug peddlers without any ethics.

Dan mumbled a "yes" as the president disconnected his phone. Dan then called KunKar and conveyed the same message to him.

As the Li sisters came me out of the cockpit, Husn and Aashiq were both alert and ready for any eventuality. They needn't have bothered because the Li sisters did not even glance at either Husn or Aashiq as they walked past them. Husn thought that she noticed a tinge of disappointment on their faces.

Intuitively, she knew that the Li sisters had been restrained from carrying out their plans. Silently, she thanked Kun Kar but decided not to take chances. She told Aashiq they needed to stay alert until they landed in Beijing. Taking the first watch, she asked him to rest until it was time for his turn. To keep herself from falling asleep, she focused on staying sharp and attentive to the task. She was eager to visit the Wuhan Institute of Virology, established in 1956, and even more excited to see China's first biosafety level 4 (BSL-4) lab, which had been operational at the institute since 2015.

Husn had burnt the internet to read all about WVI and Coronavirus and was aware that various viruses were being researched there, and pharmaceutical companies were also funding studies to develop vaccines for the viruses. She had encountered several conspiracy theories: that the virus had leaked from WVI, that the Wuhan wet market was the source where it spread from bats to pangolins to humans, and that pharmaceutical companies had encouraged the virus's spread to profit from vaccines. The most intriguing theory was that China deliberately unleashed the virus to weaken the USA and surpass it as the world's top superpower.

As she wondered whether they, the duo, would be able to successfully investigate the origins of the Coronavirus, her thoughts moved to Shi Zengli, a virologist working as number two at WVI and also known as the bat woman for her extensive research on bats. Husn was keen to meet her and hoped for some help from her in getting to the bottom of the Coronavirus mystery.

As the wheels of the chartered aircraft touched down at 'Starfish', she was shaken out of her thoughts. Smiling to herself as she shook Aashiq awake, she had kept watch for all four hours, having forgotten to wake Aashiq up!

Aashiq broke out of his deep slumber, completely refreshed.

Husn brain texted their arrival to Sonny and Vidya, who were still cooped up in the US Embassy.

Next, she texted Kun Kar, who invited both of them to join him for a late dinner and spend the night at his residence before catching the morning train to Wuhan. A shiver went down her spine again as she read Kun Kar's message and steeled herself to tackle the situation as it unfolded. Aashiq had regained all his energy and was his chirpy self. At the immigration, they were received by the liaison officer, and a few minutes later, they were in the car, which headed towards Kun Kar's residence. After extending the invite to the duo, Kun Kar went in for a bath; he wanted to be at his best tonight.

In the car to Kun Kar's residence, Aashiq read about the India–China standoff in Ladakh, and he texted Vidya seeking details.

Vidya replied, saying that he had been following the news for the last 48 hours, and he summarised it for Aashiq: the Chinese had crossed the Line of Actual Control (LAC) at four places in Eastern Ladakh and had occupied vantage points inside the Indian territory claiming it as their own. Hectic military and diplomatic parlays followed, which led to the withdrawal of troops from both sides.

Two Indian patrols, out to check on the Chinese withdrawal, found them still in the Indian territory. Fisticuffs, pushing, stone-throwing, and beating with iron rods followed. Reportedly, the area was a narrow ridge, and some troops were pushed into the gorge. Both sides suffered casualties: Indians announced one Colonel and twenty-one troops dead, and the Chinese confirmed casualties but were mum on the numbers.

Vidya added that different perceptions of the LAC were the underlying cause for such actions, but India, while it wanted friendly relations with China, was unlikely to buckle under pressure.

Vidya went on, "Given China's recent assertiveness toward Taiwan, Vietnam, Hong Kong, the South China

Sea, and the Philippines, could China be falling into the Thucydides Trap?" Aashiq smiled when he read the mention of the Thucydides Trap. He knew that 90 percent of their colleagues would have Googled it. The theory suggests that when a rising power threatens to overtake an established one, war is often the outcome.

He was about to reply when Husn told him that they were about to reach Kun Kar's residence.

Kun Kar lived in a well-appointed double-storied mansion in Zhongnanhai, an exclusive area which housed the top leadership of the Politburo Standing Committee. It was closed to the general public after the Tiananmen Square protests of 1989. Kun Kar, a confirmed bachelor, had a picturesque view of the lake from his first-floor bedroom. He had planned to spend the evening with Husn, sipping wine and enjoying the serene beauty of the moonlit lake, while making love to her. Kun Kar, like Chairman Mao, had a voracious appetite for sex.

Kun Kar walked to the foyer as the car carrying the duo came to a halt on the porch. Husn and Aashiq came out of the rear seats, picked up their bags from the boot, and moved to the foyer. They were both putting on face masks, as Kun Kar was; a few cases of Coronavirus infections had been reported in Beijing in the last couple of days.

They exchanged bows from a distance. Kun Kar was drawn to Husn and wanted to hug her but controlled himself, knowing that they would be together after dinner.

Welcoming them, KunKar offered them a drink, which they refused, saying that they were both very hungry. He asked them to join him in the dining room after freshening up.

Fifteen minutes later, they were all at the dining table. Kun Kar took care to cater to Aashiq's tastes, and mutton biryani was served to him. Aashiq's eyes lit up, and thanking Kun Kar for being such a good host and serving him his favourite dish, he dug into it. For Husn, Kun Kar had Chinese delicacies laid out: there were fried bee pupae, wormwood dumplings, stinky tofu, spicy frog stem, and Wonton soup.

As they ate, Kun Kar, in fluent English, briefed them on their mission. He was upfront in telling them that China was under pressure to investigate the origin and spread of Coronavirus. The Chinese were clear that they were not involved in any way. The president was keen to clear the air and had chosen Husn and Aashiq to carry out the investigations to lend credibility to the findings.

Next, he briefly mentioned the theories doing the rounds: the possibility of a manmade Coronavirus being released in the Wuhan wet market and suspected sabotage by one of the hundred-plus foreign scientists working in the WVI. He asked Aashiq to do as Husn told him because she was well-versed in the language and local customs. What he didn't tell him was that Husn was one of them, nurtured since her childhood, and she would be more loyal to the motherland than to her family. She was expected to get to the truth but only inform Kun Kar. Aloud, he informed them that he had already spoken to both the director and the bat woman, and they would provide all help in the investigations.

In Chinese, he told Husn that there was a section in the institute which was known only to the Director, bat woman, and select Chinese scientists. He asked her to avoid mentioning it, let alone planning to visit it. Husn politely suggested that, to maintain secrecy and ensure a thorough investigation, only she could be permitted access to that section. Anticipating Kun Kar's question, she added that she could keep Aashiq away from this restricted area, although she herself knew little about it.

Without contesting Husn's request, Kun Kar smoothly slipped back into English, asking Aashiq how the lamb biryani was. Aashiq's reply was an appreciative nod as he continued to wolf it down with periodic gulps of coke. Husn requested a preserved egg, and the dinner was almost over with no dessert being served other than chocolates, which were kept on the table.

Husn thanked Kun Kar for the lovely dinner, mentioning that she and Aashiq had an early train to catch, and stood up from the table. Aashiq followed her lead. Kun Kar remained seated and offered them chamomile tea, which they both declined. Wishing them goodnight, Kun Kar then spoke to Husn in Chinese, asking her to come to his room in fifteen minutes. Although Aashiq didn't understand Chinese, he sensed the implication. Once they were out of earshot, he asked Husn what she planned to do. He'd noticed the lust in Kun Kar's eyes. Husn simply smiled, reassuring Aashiq not to worry—she knew ways to manage Kun Kar without provoking him. Aashiq went into his room very worried; KunKar's look was still haunting him.

Husn went into her room, took off her clothes, bathed, perfumed herself, put on her nightie, and knocked at Kun Kar's door. She was clear in her mind; Kun Kar was an influential member of the most powerful committee in the country, and she had to have him eating out of her hand.

"Come in," Kun Kar called, his voice catching slightly in his throat with nervous excitement. Husn opened the door and stepped into a spacious room with a king-size bed and a stunning view of the lake. Kun Kar stood there wearing only a black robe that fell just to his knees, discreetly concealing his paunch.

His heartbeat quickened as he saw Husn. He got up from his wing chair and walked quickly up to Husn to give her a bear hug. Before he could do that, his mobile rang. The ringtone froze Kun Kar in his tracks: it was the president calling. Kun Kar knew the president lived in Beijing's Central District, so he had brought the duo to his own residence in Zhongnanhai. However, what Kun Kar didn't realize was that Dan's team closely monitored every senior party official, reporting anything unusual directly to the president. The president was promptly informed of the duo's overnight stay at Kun Kar's residence, raising his suspicions about his motives. When the President called to confirm, the irritation and fear in Kun Kar's voice immediately told him that Husn was indeed with KunKar.

The president smiled as he realised Kun Kar's predicament. Aloud, in a no-nonsense tone, he asked if Husn was with him. Kun Kar, who had frozen like a deer in searchlights, whispered in the affirmative. The president told him that Husn was an invaluable asset and he should let her get some sleep before boarding the train early the next morning. Kun Kar could barely mumble a yes before the president cut the call. Kun Kar felt all the energy drain out of his body as he sank into his wing chair.

Husn couldn't hear the other person's voice on Kun Kar's mobile but could guess that it was the president; none other, she thought, could reduce Kun Kar from a raging bull to a frightened kitten. Turning towards Kun Kar, she asked him if he needed water. Kun Kar shook his head in reply and told her that the president was on the line and had tasked him with some urgent work.

"Fine," said Husn, "I better be going then," and turned to leave. Kun Kar told her that they would meet again, just the two of them, and bid her good night. As she pulled open the door to go to her bedroom, Kun Kar, in a loud enough voice, told her that he would remain her guardian angel and that a call from her would be sufficient in case of any adversity faced by her.

Husn knew that Kun Kar was the ace up her sleeve as long as he was besotted with her. Back in her room, she found Aashiq pacing up and down. He appeared relieved to see Husn back and safe. Husn, all smiles, told him that the 'supreme leader' had come to her rescue as she bid him good night.

Chapter 6

Delaying the Inevitable

Norman received a call from the Big Circle Gang safe house in Beijing. He was told that the assassination had to be postponed on the express request of Dan, the Chief of the Chinese Internal Security Service who had also conveyed that the duo could be taken out after they had completed their mission.

Norman was upset but didn't show it. The caller told Norman that the advance money would be returned. Norman told the caller to keep the advance as the assassination had only been postponed and instructed him to keep the target under close surveillance and neutralise the duo on clearance from Dan. After the call, Norman thought long and hard: ideally, the duo should have been kept away from the WVI, and if they did pay a visit to the institute, they had to be kept away from the R & D section, which was working on the Coronavirus vaccine.

He decided to call another meeting of the head honchos of the pharma majors and picked up his mobile.

Suddenly an idea struck him and instead of coordinating the meeting, he decided to call the Chief Executive Officer of Shanghai Pharmaceuticals, a 5 billion dollar pharmaceutical giant headquartered in Shanghai. Liu, the CEO, immediately picked up Norman's call and both spoke for over ten minutes. Norman narrated the whole story regarding Husn and Aashiq and requested Liu to ensure that the duo was kept away from WVI and definitely from its R&D section.

Liu was part of the long-term plan of the pharma majors: develop a virus and its vaccine simultaneously in the R&D section of WVI so that in case of a pandemic, the pharmaceutical companies could sing their way to the banks by manufacturing and selling the vaccine.

In most technologically advanced countries, laws on developing viruses in the labs amounted to manufacturing a biological weapon and were explicitly forbidden. So the pharma majors had focused on the Wuhan institute, though a safety level four lab but not constrained by strict norms or oversight, funding it generously and stationing its scientists there knowing that the biological weapons regime was neither as specific nor as strict in that part of the world. The Chinese government was happy with the funding and the cutting-edge R&D being carried out as it provided the latest technical know-how.

In private, the Chinese president had stated clearly that technology was synonymous with power; therefore, China had to be on the forefront of the technological world. That the Chinese government intentionally turned a blind eye to the goings-on in the WVI or was blissfully ignorant was a matter of conjecture.

What Liu was clearly aware of was that the Chinese government was under pressure domestically because of a faltering economy and unrest in Hong Kong, Tibet, and Xin Xiang province. To add to its woes, it had been driven into a corner because of the alleged origin of the Coronavirus in the Wuhan wet market. Liu also knew that his country's efforts to distract its people through a standoff with India in Eastern Ladakh, threatening Taiwan through repeated airspace violations by its bomber aircraft, and bullying the South China Sea littorals had all boomeranged. Australia had, in fact, pointedly blamed China for a cyber-attack on its facilities. Liu understood that the Chinese government could ill afford any negative news, especially regarding Coronavirus.

Liu listened to Norman and told him that the order not to harm Husn and Aashiq would have come from the very top, meaning the president himself. Liu said that it appeared the president was keen to project to the world that the virus had not originated from the WVI based on an audit by a team of WAP whiz kids. Till now, the Chinese had balked at any inquiry being carried out at the WVI, which had given rise to rumours of Chinese complicity in manufacturing and spreading the virus across the world. However, a favourable audit report would scotch all rumours and Husn, who in all probability, had already been briefed appropriately by the Chinese government, would ensure that. And the western world would buy it because of Husn's antecedents, opined Liu.

Having explained the issue to Norman, Liu said that trying to stop Husn and Aashiq from visiting the institute would not be prudent, but he would definitely try to prevent them from visiting the R&D section.

As Norman thanked Liu and expressed his gratitude, Liu disconnected the call and dialled the bat woman. He knew that she would be able to prevent the duo from entering the R&D section more effectively than the director himself: she was a strong, no-nonsense, ambitious Han and a dyed-in-the-wool communist. Liu knew her for the last 15 years and it helped that she got a very healthy monthly grant in aid from Shanghai Pharma Corporation.

Just as Shi Zhangli was about to sit down for dinner, Liu's call came through. Aware of her short temper and dislike for interruptions, he began with a sincere apology and stressed the urgency of the matter. Although initially irritated, Shi appreciated Liu's efficiency and, putting aside her annoyance, asked him to proceed. Liu then briefed her on the duo, their mission at WVI, the potential risk to the vaccine, and the disastrous consequences that could unfold if it were compromised.

Shi spoke over Liu as he dropped the names of Dan, Kun Kar, and the president. He told him to breathe easily as she already knew about the duo's visit and the dire need to keep the vaccine a secret. She told Liu that Kun Kar had already called the director and briefed him about the visit of the duo and the unfettered access to be provided to them. The director, as usual, had delegated the responsibility to her, and she had already chalked out the broad contours of their visit.

In their itinerary, Shi confirmed there was no visit to the R&D section, and she would stonewall all attempts by the duo in case a request was made to visit it. Liu now breathed easy, confident that Shi would be able to keep the duo away from the R&D section.

At around the same time, the Li sisters had eaten their frugal dinner of pork chow mein and were being briefed about their task by number two of the Beijing unit of the Big Circle Gang. They were both very happy that they would be permitted to eliminate the duo in due course. They had a one hundred percent success rate in taking out targets and dearly wanted to maintain it. They were told to keep the duo under close surveillance starting from their train journey to Wuhan early the next morning and to kill them upon receiving orders from the Big Circle Gang.

Because the duo had seen them as air hostesses, they were to travel and stay separately, change their appearances to chic Beijing girls visiting Wuhan, and take extra care not to raise any suspicions in the mind of the duo. They were to follow the duo to and from the WVI but were not to enter it unless ordered to.

The sisters, professional as ever, packed all their stuff and were ready to get into their beds within thirty minutes of their briefing.

'ICE LILIES'

"Check," said Tanya and gave a pitying look at Sonny; he was wondering if it was a good decision to contact the 'Ice Lilies' after all.

In about half an hour of contacting them, they had found out about the mission of the four WAP nerds and the trouble they were in & were even keen to help with the solutions! Before Tanya could say 'mate', Sonny told her that he would discuss it with his partner, Vidya, and get back in about an hour.

Sonny appeared frustrated as he told Vidya that contacting the 'Ice Lilies' was a mistake which he shouldn't have committed. Giving a reassuring smile, Vidya asked Sonny to take deep breaths for two minutes and narrate in detail about the 'Ice Lilies' and his relationship with them. Only then could he confirm if Sonny was in the wrong for contacting the 'Ice Lilies'!

Sonny told Vidya that he had met the 'Ice Lilies' in Amsterdam in the summer of 2018 when he had decided to lose himself in the smoke-filled cafes to overcome an emotional breakup.

On his fourth day of the vacation, he was sitting in a café, all by himself, smoking a joint, when Tanya walked up to him, introduced herself, and sat down. About five feet eight inches tall, she had long and straight brown hair, blue eyes, and long legs. Dressed in halters and hot pants, she looked very chic and had the incredibly upright posture of the female Russian tennis stars. Her eyes gave her away; she was physically attracted to Sonny and was chatting away to hide her excitement.

Sonny had faced such situations earlier and knew that girls invariably fell for his boyish good looks and lifeguard's body. He gently told her that he was gay and saw the disappointment in her eyes. Nevertheless, she chatted for a few minutes and then excused herself. Sonny lit another joint, took a deep drag, and felt the smoke enter his lungs and calm his mind. He closed his eyes, hoping to fully relax, when he heard a new voice—it was Anita, greeting him with a bold "hello." She didn't mince words, quickly admitting that she and her friend Tanya had a wager on who would lay him first.

Sonny smiled in spite of himself. He hadn't faced this situation earlier. He asked Anita to call Tanya to the table and advised them to put the bet off because it was technically not feasible! Instead, he offered his friendship to them and once a rapport was struck, he had poured his heart out to them about why he was in Amsterdam and what he did for a living.

'Ice Lilies' hearts melted upon hearing Sonny's break up, and they promised that they would help him overcome his sorrow. They got him high on joints, took him boating in the canals and cycling across the city, and also made him dance his blues away in the all-night discotheques.

They also shared their personal stories. Both were born in Sevastopol, a port city on the Black Sea, and grew up amidst an active separatist movement against Ukraine. This movement culminated in the annexation of the Crimean Peninsula by Russia in 2014, which included Sevastopol. Since the majority of the population was East Slavic and spoke Russian, a referendum was held, where 95 percent of the voters, out of 83 percent of the population who cast their ballots, voted in favor of joining Russia.

Being born and brought up in a city which was part of Muslim territory till 1921, when the Soviet Republic took over and then in 1934 became a part of Ukraine and finally Russian territory in 2014, gave them sharper survival instincts. Schooling was tough because of the ongoing unrest, but both of them, being studious and hardworking, did well and moved to Moscow University for their college education. Both of them opted for information technology as their major subject, and Anita was in the second year of her studies when Tanya joined as a fresher. They met for the first time at the icebreaker party.

Being from Sevastopol, they gravitated towards each other and became good friends. Anita and Tanya also secretly became members of the Pussy Riot band, which eventually caught the attention of the feared secret police. One night, the FSB (Federal Security Service of the Russian Federation) knocked on their door with a veiled threat and an offer to recruit them as hackers. Both women knew that the FSB was even more dangerous than the KGB, so their survival instincts kicked in. They quickly abandoned their involvement with Pussy Riot and were instead initiated into the world of hacking. Six months into their hacking training, they got their moniker 'IceLilies': cold like ice and beautiful like lilies.

As they trained together, they became inseparable, and the virtual world became their real world. A year later, they were participating in hackathons and winning them. Their performances were noted by FSB, and they were brought in to influence the US elections. Their success got them more such projects from the FSB and also their patronage.

'IceLilies' were fast becoming influencers in the real world as well as on the darknet. Slowly, they realised the power they were starting to wield. They could hack into anything and everything across the globe, and they could do it without raising any alarms. Their Modus operandi was many times more effective than the so-called cyber-attacks, which appeared to be amateurish chest-thumping in comparison.

However, as sensible girls of Sevastopol, they did not change their lifestyle or take to fancy cars and expensive minks. Instead, they requested the FSB to assist them in enrolling as students for a master's degree programme at the Amsterdam University of Applied Sciences.

They knew that Amsterdam, with its liberal laws and legalised weed, was a hackers' paradise, and they wanted to escape the cruel cold of Moscow. So they were in Amsterdam for the last two and a half years, living like students on a shoestring budget. At the same time, they had hundreds of bitcoins in their account. The only hobby they permitted themselves was playing the 'Make Friends with Male Strangers' challenge.

FSB knew about their hobby, but realising their value as hackers, it overlooked their sole indiscretion and provided them with covert physical protection. FSB also told them not to carry out any disruptive act in the cyber world independently; this always rankled with 'Ice Lilies' because they felt shackled.

"Now, within minutes of contacting 'Ice Lilies', they know all about our mission, team composition, tasking, and also our tribulations and are keen to offer solutions too while we have been sworn to secrecy by the president of WAP," Sonny explained to Vidya with an exasperated look. By now, Vidya was clear about the capabilities of the 'Ice Lilies'. He told Sonny that 'Ice Lilies' could be of help in accomplishing their mission and asked him to shoot off an email to President WAP telling all about 'Ice Lilies', help they could render, and that they wouldn't be told anything about the mission that they already did not know.

Sonny smiled, thanked Vidya and shot off an email to President WAP. In a couple of minutes, he received a reply which said, 'Go ahead but tell them nothing of which they know not.' Sonny sighed in relief, sent an acknowledgement and connected with 'Ice Lilies' on VOIP.

Before Sonny could say hello, Tanya shouted, "Check Mate," and Sonny raised his hands in mock surrender. He told them that they should work out a plan to get him and Vidya out of the US Embassy.

With a very straight face, Anita replied, "We will, Sonny, as long as you don't tell us anything of which we know not," and both she and Tanya burst out laughing.

Sonny was both astonished and aghast as he realised that they had hacked into his email account.

"My little bee," said Anita, "We have not hacked into your email account; we are just maintaining it so that it does not get targeted by a Trojan Horse or phishing attacks." "To do that", she added, "we have to check and see through all your emails." Sonny shook his head in mock disgust and told them that they were hiding in the US Embassy because of the Chinese assassin but needed to get out and visit the San Siro Stadium.

'Ice Lilies' asked Sonny to describe in detail their movements after landing at the Schiphol Airport. They also asked him to describe the Chinese assassin, including the disguise that he had used to fool them. Sonny took his time describing everything in detail, especially the Chinese assassin. 'Ice Lilies' listened in rapt silence, and once he finished, they told him that they would be back with a plan soon. After disconnecting the call, Sonny asked Vidya if they could work on the application brain texted by Aashiq.

Vidya agreed and told Sonny that it would be better if they discussed and kept refining the application in their brain because no amount of firewalls and air gaps could keep it safe from hackers. Sonny readily agreed because he was still hurting: the way his email account was hacked into by the 'Ice Lilies' was an abject humiliation. He also understood that no information or data was safe in the cyber world.

For the next two hours, they worked on the Coronavirus application software and the closer they got to a failsafe solution, the more animated they became. They were keen to complete the prototype before the day was over, but a call from Anita disrupted their plans of completing the prototype. She confirmed that they were able to identify the Chinese assassin in a matter of minutes by hacking into the cameras at the Schiphol Airport, at the hostel, and at the restaurant. "And once we have a photograph of a person," piped in Tanya, "we find out more about him than the person himself or his parents know about him."

'IceLilies' had hacked into the passport and visa office, driving licence, and income tax offices of the complete EU, USA, China, and South East and East Asian countries. Through machine learning tools, the comparison of the photo and identification of the person was done in quick time, and thereafter AI tools were manipulated to get all the details possible about him. It was established that he was Brussels-based, worked in the Chinese embassy there but actually was on the payroll of the Chinese Internal Security Service. In fact, he was one of their valued agents who was a polyglot, master of disguise, and a deadly assassin. With some more effort, they were able to get hold of his call data records, WeChat and VOIP records.

These details helped them thread the whole plot. It was the Chinese who were after Sonny and Vidya. They knew about the duo's mission and were very keen that the elimination of the duo took place before their visit to the San Siro Stadium. The assassin had been instructed by the boss of the Chinese internal secret service to take them out within a couple of hours of their landing at Schiphol Airport, and the assassin had never missed his prey earlier, so they were lucky to be still alive.

As Sonny gave a wry grin, Anita told him that the threat was far from over and that the assassin who was working in the embassy was keeping a watch over them; the moment they stepped out of the embassy, the assassin would be lying in wait for them. Sonny told them that the CIA station chief had advised that they move to the airport in a helicopter which he would arrange and take the first flight to the USA. "However," said Sonny, "they had been specifically instructed to visit the San Siro Stadium and pick up clues, if any, and they would like to do so if it was possible."

Anita smiled and said, "My little bee, we will arrange your visit to the pope if you so desire," and added that a plan had already been worked out for them.

On hearing the word 'plan', both Sonny and Vidya were all ears and listened to Anita with undivided attention as she unfolded it.

Chapter 7

In the Mouth of the Dragon

Aashiq was dreaming of 'Gushtaba', a Kashmiri delicacy: tender meatballs cooked in flavourful yogurt gravy, when his mobile's alarm rang. Aashiq loved his sleep and hated to get up, especially in the early hours of the morning. He dragged himself out of bed and called Husn as he entered the bathroom to get ready.

She was already awake, practising meditation. Of all the exercises and regimens taught to her by her parents, she found meditation and Pranayama to be the most effective. She practised both daily, and if her schedule was too tight, she would do one of them every alternate day. She found that the meditation-pranayama combo helped her remain calm, energetic, creative and happy.

She looked at Dalai Lama, the political, religious and spiritual leader of the Tibetans who was forced to flee his native land, as her inspiration. He always maintained his calm and endearing smile in the face of periodic humiliation and name-calling by the Chinese government. His aura blessed millions as he searched for peace for his people.

Fifteen minutes later, they were in the car, which dropped them off at the Beijing West railway station at 06:30 hours. Their train, G 507, a high speed bullet train, departed as scheduled at 06:53 hours. They had been booked in business class and had already been served their welcome drink as the train moved soundlessly with a small tug and increased its speed to 150 kilometres per hour. It would arrive at Wuhan at 12:24 hours, covering an approximate distance of 1200 plus kilometres in five and a half hours. For most of the journey, it would be cruising at a speed of 250 kilometres per hour.

Aashiq was ravenously hungry and ordered an American breakfast of fried eggs, , fruits, porridge, bread, and coffee. Husn ordered fresh fruit juice and half-boiled eggs. As they sipped their coffee, Husn told Aashiq about her post-dinner meeting with Kun Kar. Aashiq laughed as he heard the bit about Kun Kar turning ashen-faced upon receiving the president's call. He commented that Kun Kar would think twice before trying to get fresh with her in the future.

Husn smiled and turned her head to look out of the window to contemplate in silence as emerald-green paddy fields whizzed by, but Aashiq's snoring startled her out of her reverie. The American breakfast had made him feel full and sleepy , and he had fallen fast asleep within a minute of finishing his coffee. Husn gently held his chin and moved his face slightly, and Aashiq's snoring stopped; this was a trick taught by her mother which she used to good effect to stop her husband's dreadful snoring!

Li sisters, too, were on the same train. While they slept in the same bedroom, they left for the railway station in separate cars and were seated separately on either side of the coach Husn and Aashiq were in. They had arrived earlier at the railway station and kept a discreet watch as Husn and Aashiq had arrived and boarded the train. They were now dressed as university students in jeans and tops with light jackets and Adidas campus shoes. Both of them also had a sumptuous Chinese breakfast of pork dumplings and washed it down with green tea. They had decided to keep a watch on Husn and Aashiq by turns so that they could catch up with their sleep and were careful not to expose themselves to their prey while watching over them.

Outwardly, they were petite young Chinese girls on vacation, but as thoroughbred professionals, all they were waiting for was the go-ahead. The moment they got it, their prey would die, unsuspecting and ignorant, while they would slip out unheard, unnoticed, and undetected.

Train G 507 glided into the Wuhan railway station at 12:22 hours, two minutes ahead of schedule. The director of WVI and the bat woman were present on the platform to receive the audit team. They understood the importance of getting a clean chit from this team and, therefore, didn't want to leave any stone unturned to ensure it. They got into two cars, Director with Husn and bat woman with Aashiq and moved to Hotel Shangri La, where they were booked in two separate but adjoining suites. Unknown to them, both the suites had been bugged, and the audio-visual feed was being received in a suite on the same floor booked for the Li sisters. Husn and Aashiq checked into their suites and, after a quick wash up and change, were ready to move to WVI accompanied by the Director and the bat woman.

Anita and Tanya had worked out an escape plan for Sonny and Vidya based on their hacking strengths. Sonny had contacted the CIA station chief and told him that they had dwelt and deliberated on his recommendation of getting out of Amsterdam and getting back to the US. He confirmed that though it appeared to be a softer option, finding it more pragmatic, they had decided to go back to the US.

The Station Chief was delighted. He told them that he would get their tickets booked on the first flight out to the US and provide them with a helicopter up to the airport to keep the Chinese assassin at bay. Sonny told him that their tickets had already been booked on the United Airlines flight departing at 02:00 hours; however, the helicopters could drop them at Schiphol Airport at around 23:00 hours. "Sure thing, Sonny," boomed the Station Chief, "I am so happy that you are heeding my advice and flying to safety."

The next call Sonny made was to the reception to inform them that they would be checking out in the evening and returning to the US later at night. "Would you require a vehicle to drop you at the airport, Mr. Sonny?" the receptionist asked. Thanking her, Sonny said that they wouldn't be requiring it as they would be flying to the airport in a helicopter.

Love Li's informer had left a word at the reception that he should be informed about the movement of the duo out of the embassy, so the receptionist called him and gave out the details of the duo's departure plan.

He, in turn, called Love Li and told him that a helicopter was taking the duo to Schiphol Airport at around 22:45 hours, and they were flying out later the same night to the US. Love Li was all rested, fresh, and raring to go. He deliberated on the inputs received, cross-checked the bookings on the United Airlines flights, and quickly worked out a plan to eliminate them in the embassy itself. He then called up Dan and sought his go-ahead to eliminate the duo before they boarded the helicopter.

His plan was to hide in a repair truck, get inside the embassy, enter their apartment from the top down using his Parkour skills, and wring their necks with his bare hands. He would make a quick exit in the informer's car hidden in the boot, which would be waiting about a hundred metres from the apartment. Dan listened impassively without interrupting and then asked Love Li about the authenticity of the inputs. Love Li confirmed that the credibility of his source was A1, two seats in the names of Sonny and Vidya were booked in business class on the United Airlines flight, and the helicopter's flight plan to Schiphol Airport would be reaching the ATC in an hour or so.

Dan gave his provisional go-ahead to Love Li and told him to work out the minute details of the plan to avoid any glitches. Dan added that the final confirmation will, however, be given once the ATC confirms receipt of the helicopter's flight plan. He also told Love Li to exit the country soonest after killing the duo and disguise himself as a cleaning woman for the operation. Love Li immediately understood that as a cleaning woman, there would be the least suspicion if some person or CCTV camera spotted him within the embassy premises. He also understood that the killing of the duo inside the embassy will have major repercussions internationally and the hunt for the killer will be quick and massive in scale, and police forces across the EU will join hands to ensure quick capture; therefore, the need to exit the borders at the earliest.

He replied in affirmative to Dan, bid him goodbye, called up his source in the ATC and asked to be informed immediately on receipt of the helicopter flight plan from the US Embassy. Next, he looked up the flight schedule of various international flights flying out of Schiphol Airport in the evening.

He had decided to avoid the US, the UK, and the EU altogether. Looking at flights to Asia and Africa, he homed in on a Singapore International Airport flight taking off at 22:00 hours and booked himself on it. He knew that he would be well placed to reach the airport by 20:00 hours as he planned to take out the duo earlier in the day. Also, he preferred Singapore because of the strong underground Chinese network there; once he landed at Changi Airport, he would be protected against all threats by the underground Chinese network. Within half an hour, he got a call from the ATC that the helicopter flight plan from the US Embassy had been received. It would take off at 21:45 hours and would land at Schiphol Airport at 22:05 hours. Love Li thanked him and contacted Dan on WeChat to confirm both the helicopter flight plan's receipt at the ATC, Schiphol Airport and his own getaway plan to Singapore. Dan had thought the whole plan through and, without wasting time, requested a call to the president.

The president was chairing a meeting, so Dan had to wait for fifteen minutes before he was put through. As the president came online, Dan again stood at attention and bowed slightly as he greeted him. He then updated him on the assassination plan of the nosy and meddlesome duo and strongly recommended that both of them be taken out at the embassy itself. He also said that he was fully confident that Love Li would execute the plan and get away without getting caught.

The president's gut reaction was to give the go-ahead immediately. He was fed up with the Americans and wanted blood. It appeared that suddenly, China was an evil power bullying other nations to its advantage. Accusing the Chinese of stealing the secrets of the vaccine and other technologies, the US ordered the shutting down of the Chinese consulate in Houston, the US aircraft carrier continued to carry out training exercises in the South China Sea and, how he hated the Indians; they weren't getting pushed over in Eastern Ladakh and were sucking up to the Americans and carrying out a joint naval exercise with them as a show of force against China. Their prime minister Mano Na Mano, who had pulled out all the stops in wining and dining him at the second India–China informal summit at Mallapuram, had the temerity to breathe fire against China in his speech to his soldiers in Ladakh recently.

He saw poetic justice in the killing of Sonny, an American, and Vidya, an Indian, as both their nations were causing him maximum trouble. He almost ordered Dan to go ahead with the plan but stopped himself and deliberated a little more. The duo, Sonny and Vidya, were mere pawns in the power game being played out. He would derive a lot of personal satisfaction if they were knocked off, but he also knew that carrying out the killing in the US Embassy would be in stark violation of international norms. They would be able to trace back the killings to Love Li and raise a lot of stink.

Already, China was being projected as an international bully who believed in vassal states and transactional relationships. This perception and the thought that all democracies should unite against China could prove detrimental to his motherland's quest to become the global hegemon. He also knew that any adverse external action would impact his image and standing within the party and the country.

He knew that there were still some members of the Politburo who wanted to topple him even though he had purged a large number of them on account of corruption. Seeing the larger picture and counselling himself with strategic patience, he instructed Dan, who was waiting patiently on the other side, not to carry out the hit in case the duo was returning to the US without making a visit to the San Siro Stadium. Dan mumbled a yes, and as he did so, the president told Dan to confirm the duo's arrival at the airport and their departure for the US and cut the call.

Dan called up Love Li and told him that taking out the American and the Indian was off the table. Love Li was to monitor their movements at the airport and confirm their departure to and arrival at JFK Airport, New York. Love Li was bitterly disappointed and told Dan so. He added that this would be his first failure in taking out targets successfully. Dan understood Love Li well and conveyed to him that he had not failed, but the orders for him had changed.

Telling Love Li to keep him updated regarding the movements of Sonny and Vidya, he disconnected the call.

Anita and Tanya, working in tandem, had managed to hack the mobile phones of Dan, Love Li, his informer in the US Embassy in Amsterdam and the DCM in the local Chinese embassy. They listened in on the Dan-Love Li conversation in near real-time and told Sonny and Vidya that the Chinese, in a rare show of kindness, had decided not to eliminate them as long as they boarded the US-bound flight as scheduled. Sonny bowed slightly as he mockingly thanked the Chinese president in absentia for his uncharacteristic magnanimity & asked Anita to share the details of their escape plan. Anita told them that they would reach Schiphol Airport using the embassy helicopter and check-in at the United Airlines counter at around 22:15 hours. Though the United Airlines flight was fully booked, very cleverly, after hacking into the airline's servers, their names had been added without impacting the total. They would be issued boarding passes, pass through the immigration office, and head towards the departure lounge. The Chinese assassin would be able to monitor them physically up to the immigration area and thereafter would move to the ATC to confirm the take-off.

Both Sonny and Vidya were to move to the restroom once the boarding gate opened and the passengers started getting into the aircraft. In the restroom, they were to change into airport janitors' uniforms, which they would be given at the embassy itself along with the airport entry/exit passes; a friend of 'Ice Lilies' would deliver both items to them by 20:00 hours. Having changed into the janitors' uniforms, they, on confirmation from 'Ice Lilies', would exit the airport from gate number 18, from where they would be picked up by 'Ice Lilies' in their beaten-up Lada car.

As Sonny started to thank them, Tanya, in mock seriousness, said that they would extract their pound of 'flesh', and Vidya howled in mock fright even as Sonny told the 'Ice Lilies' that they would be good to go as per the plan laid out for them.

Two hours later, Mike Pompoi, the US Secretary of State, well known for his strong anti-China views and called 'Evil' by the Chinese, put a photograph of his golden Retriever pup, Mercer, playing with his toys. In the centre of all the toys lay Winnie the Pooh. This photograph was seen by the Chinese president and his blood boiled.

He was derisively known as Winnie the Pooh amongst his own people, and he hated it so much that he banned *Winnie the Pooh* movies in China. To add insult to injury, Winnie the Pooh was lying on his back, all helpless and at the mercy of Mercer, the pup.

As he was trying to calm himself down, his strategic adviser came in to inform him that the FBI had accused the Chinese consulate in San Francisco of harbouring Tang Juan, a Chinese researcher, who was charged in federal court in California regarding her military background.

The president had already ordered the closure of the US Consulate in Chengdu as a reaction to the closure of the Chinese consulate in Houston, but the combination of Grump-Pompoi appeared to be hell-bent on damaging bilateral relations and the Chinese economy. The dark desire of revenge, strong and intense, rose inside him.

He asked to be connected to Dan. Within minutes, Dan was online, and the president, without bothering to exchange pleasantries, told Dan to kill the duo at the airport before they boarded their flight. Dan knew better than to inquire into the sudden change of orders. He, on the contrary, was happy for Love Li, who would be able to maintain his hundred percent hit record.

He called Love Li on WeChat, who was overjoyed on hearing that the duo was to be taken out. His hands itched to break their necks, and his impassive face glowed with excitement. However, when Dan was asked about the modus operandi, he said that he would use poisonous darts to hit the necks of the targets when they were at the check-in or at the immigration counter. He had realised that though wringing their necks would give him more pleasure, the chances of his being caught were higher. In the case of poisonous darts, he would fire them from a distance, avoiding the CCTV cameras as much as feasible and in the guise of an air hostess.

He would move to the nearest washroom after firing the poisonous darts, change into the guise of the homosexual poet, and exit the airport. "Why at the check-in or the immigration counter," inquired Dan, "that's because the targets would be close to each other, and I would be able to fire two of the darts accurately in quick succession," Love Li replied.

Love Li then told Dan he would try to create a blip in the CCTV recording at the time of the firing of the poisonous darts so that the Chinese air hostess was not caught in the act by the CCTV camera. He would be in Brussels before the air hostess was spotted as a suspect, and border check posts were alerted. Dan okayed his plan and instructed him to drive straight to Brussels after the hit.

Sonny received a call from Anita and, in typical dark Russian humour, she told him that their death warrant had just been signed and they better let her know their last wish, which she would try to fulfil. Sonny smiled and asked her to elaborate: she narrated Love Li's new plan to Sonny verbatim. Vidya, who was listening in, mockingly pleaded with Anita to help save them from the evil clutches of the Chinese. On hearing Vidya, Tanya perked up and told him that she would save him from all dangers as she wanted to taste his flesh before the Chinese consigned him to heaven. As they all laughed, Anita laid out the plan for them: she started by saying that she suspected the involvement of the top echelon of the Chinese hierarchy the way Love Li had received orders from Dan, the Chinese Chief of the dirty services department.

It appeared that he was taking orders from somebody else, and that could only be the politburo committee or Winnie the Pooh. Next, she said that the original escape plan for the duo would hold with one add-on, and that would be to tip off the airport security regarding the Chinese air hostess who would be picked up for a search. The search would yield a female man and, of course, the poisonous darts. The latter would be enough to take Love Li into custody and move him to Amsterdam for questioning. IceLilies would hack into his mobile and disable it for a few hours after his arrest so that he wouldn't be able to speak with Dan.

Sonny and Vidya would, as planned, get out of the airport as janitors from gate number 18 at the appointed time. Sonny said that he would request the CIA station chief to tip off the airport security. Anita told him to ensure that the Chinese air hostess got picked up at the right time lest Love Li dispatched them heavenwards. Sonny called up the CIA station chief and requested that the Chinese air hostess be arrested before they reached the check-in counter. The station chief, in his Texan drawl, confirmed that the Chinese air hostess would be picked up as requested.

The helicopter took off from the US Embassy at 21:45 hours with Sonny and Vidya and landed at Schiphol Airport at 22:05 hours. They were at the United Airlines check-in counter at 22:15 hours.

Love Li, in the guise of a Chinese air hostess, had reached the airport at 21:00 hours. He carried out a recce of the check-in counter area and the immigration area. He selected a firing spot in both areas, which would give him a clear view of his targets and also avoid the CCTV cameras as much as possible. He also tied up for CCTV cameras to blip at his request through a Chinese-origin local working in the CCTV control room. At 22:00 hours, as the Chinese air hostess stood looking at the electronic flight schedule board, she was tapped by a policewoman and politely asked to come with her. Love Li was taken aback and fought the impulse to flee as he saw a policeman cover him from the other side. His body search revealed his actual gender and four poisonous darts. He was taken to the central Police station in Amsterdam. He was permitted to make a call from his mobile, and he dialled Dan but couldn't get through. He requested to use the central police station phone and called up the DCM of the Chinese embassy, who reached the police station within the hour.

Love Li told him that there was definitely a leak in the plan and that he, the DCM, should inform Dan immediately. DCM returned to the embassy and called Dan in Beijing from a secure line. Dan didn't answer, and the DCM left a voicemail.

As the boarding started for the United Airlines flight to New York, Sonny and Vidya moved to the washroom, changed into janitors' uniforms at a leisurely pace, and moved towards gate No. 18. From the corner of their eyes; they also registered that the boarding of passengers on the United Airlines flight to New York was complete. They moved out of gate No. 18, were picked up by 'Ice Lilies', and taken to their apartment on the university campus.

Welcoming the two janitors to the 'IceLilies' humble abode, Anita told them to get some sleep as they planned to hit the road at 06:00 hours and reach the San Siro Stadium at 08:30 hours, which was the earliest for a visitor to be allowed inside it. "She was keen," she said, "that they visit the San Siro Stadium before the Chinese realised that they had been duped." Vidya looked at his watch, which showed that it was well past midnight. He decided to hit the sack immediately and advised Sonny to do the same to get the maximum sleep possible. Both he and Sonny were sound asleep within five minutes of hitting their beds. 'Ice Lilies', too, went to bed without further ado, knowing that they had to be fresh for the drive.

Dan returned the DCM's call and was told about Love Li's arrest. Not having received a call from Love Li, Dan was already worried and was half expecting some disappointing news, but his arrest was worse than disappointing.

Dan's mind raced as he thought quickly. He needed to put a positive spin on the report he had to send to the president. He told the DCM to check if Sonny and Vidya had boarded the United Airlines flight they were booked on. He also asked him to investigate how airport security had discovered Love Li. While he agreed with the DCM's suggestion to release Love Li without charges, he emphasized the need to find out Sonny and Vidya's current whereabouts as soon as possible.

'IceLilies', along with Sonny and Vidya, started at 06:00 hours and reached the San Siro Stadium at 08:30 hours as planned. They had booked a tour of the San Siro Stadium and were taken around by Dino, a greying, handsome 45-year-old ex-footballer. They were checked for the Coronavirus and requested to put on sanitised masks and suits before commencing the tour. To his surprise, there was a decent crowd for the tour. However, the 'Ice Lilies' had already caught Dino's attention. They asked if he could arrange for a security staff member to show them to the washroom and have them join the tour later. Dino agreed, and the four of them, along with a security guard, made their way to the nearest washroom.

As the security person waited for them, Tanya offered him a weed. He looked around, moved right below the CCTV camera to avoid being photographed and took three or four long drags. As the security guard felt lightheaded and a blissful smile spread on his lips, Tanya requested him to take them to the Central Security Control Room located in the basement to have a look-see. By now, the security guard was sold on Tanya, who was holding his arm, and asked them to follow him.

On reaching the Central Security Control Room, Anita chatted with the supervisor, who was happy that he had some visitors; he confirmed that they were probably the third or the fourth group of visitors in the last couple of years. As Sonny and Vidya looked around, Tanya got hold of the microfilm recording of the fateful Game Zero, downloaded it on her mobile, and placed the microfilm back. She then transferred the recording from her mobile phone to her laptop, which was kept in the hostel apartment. The moment she was done, she said that she was keen to return and join the tour party.

Dino saw them rejoin and realised that they had gone for a long, but Tanya's dazzling smile made him forget his concerns as he cheerfully conducted them through the stadium. Vidya filmed the seating areas, the ground, the teams' locker rooms, and the tunnels through which the players emerged for the game. They skipped the visit to the museum and drove back to Amsterdam. They were back in their hostel apartment by 13:00 hours.

As Sonny volunteered to rustle up ham sandwiches for lunch, the other three crowded in front of the laptop to watch the recording of Game Zero by the CCTV cameras installed inside the San Siro Stadium. Sonny first prepared two vegetable and cheese sandwiches because he knew how particular Vidya was about the knife being used for his vegetarian sandwiches first!

The DCM called his counterpart at the Russian embassy, a close friend, and made two requests. First, he asked him to confirm whether Sonny and Vidya, who held US and Indian passports, respectively, had flown to New York on a United Airlines flight the previous night. Second, he inquired about the reason the police had detained Love Li at Schiphol Airport. The DCM knew that his Russian counterpart was resourceful and, more importantly, wielded strong influence in Amsterdam. It took the Russian DCM about forty-five minutes to find out and call back. He confirmed that Sonny and Vidya had checked in at 22:15 hours and had flown out later in the night to New York. Regarding Love Li's apprehension, he was picked up on an anonymous tip-off received at 20:00 hours on the email of the airport police control room.

It spoke of a Chinese man masquerading as a Chinese air hostess and carrying poisonous darts with the intention of carrying out a targeted killing. The DCM thanked his Russian counterpart profusely and called up Dan on WeChat. Dan picked up on the second ring, and DCM gave him the inputs as the Russian told him. Skeptical to begin with, Dan was convinced after hearing that both the inputs were provided by DCM's opposite number in the Russian embassy in Amsterdam. Dan also knew about the Russian's influence in Amsterdam.

He decided to call up the president to give him an update. The president was on line fifteen minutes later. Dan went through the procedure of standing in attention, bowing slightly, and mumbling a greeting. The president asked Dan to fill him in with the latest. Dan explained the situation to him, outlining the arrest of Love Li, as well as the expectation of him to be released without charges. And also a report on Sonny and Vidya, who boarded their flight to New York. He also mentioned that Love Li was expected to be released without charges. In reply, Dan was expecting a mouthful from the president, but the president was calm and collected, though a little abrupt. He told Dan to ensure Love Li's release without any charges and also find out the source of the anonymous tip-off as only he, the president, and Dan knew about Love Li's plan.

Dan mumbled "yes" into the mouthpiece as the president hung up and broke into a sweat. Was the president hinting at a leak from him as Love Li definitely wouldn't have given himself away? He decided to get in touch with Love Li and get to the bottom of the issue as soon as possible. He dialled the DCM's number on WeChat.

Back at the hostel apartment, Vidya realised that they had to watch more than 20 CCTV camera recordings for two hours each. So, he suggested that they watch the recordings on separate laptops and in separate pairs. All four agreed, and Sonny and Anita started watching on her laptop while Vidya teamed up with Tanya. Vidya also suggested that they watch the recordings in fast-forward mode and pause to re-watch at normal speed if anything interesting was noticed.

They watched twelve recordings, six on each laptop, in ninety-odd minutes. It was the thirteenth CCTV camera recording in which Vidya noticed the group of East Asian spectators huddling together. He requested Tanya to play the recording at normal speed while he focused on the group that he had spotted. They appeared to be normal spectators and seemed to be enjoying the game as it progressed.

Tanya was getting impatient and asked Vidya if he wanted the mode to be switched to fast-forward. Vidya shook his head and kept his focus on the East Asians. During the half-time break, he noticed all of them get up and watched them troop towards the restroom until they got out of the camera's view. For some time, he continued watching the recording and then suddenly, on a hunch, asked Tanya to reverse and replay the recording from just before the half-time break. He also requested that she keep her eyes peeled and watch for clues regarding their investigation.

This time, both of them watched the group get up and move towards the restroom. They also noticed the man in the trench coat took something out of his pocket, put it in his mouth, and tried to light it. This time, Tanya herself touched the 'Pause' button, reversed the recording, and started viewing the action of the man in the trench coat frame-by-frame. As they watched the frame-by-frame shots, both Vidya and Tanya spotted the cigar slipping out of the fingers of Mr Trench coat while he just walked on as if nothing had happened. They sensed that something was amiss and called over Sonny and Anita to watch the recording. Vidya, in the meantime, got hold of the CCTV camera recording, which showed this group moving out of the stadium instead of returning to their seats.

Having watched the recording at normal speed, they were convinced that Mr Trench-coat was up to something and focused on him frame-by-frame. Anita finally said that it appeared that Mr Trench-coat did not have any special love for cigars and purposely let it slip from his fingers. Tanya added that Mr Trench-coat did not even spare a glance at the fallen cigar, let alone trying to retrieve it. Vidya's lips rounded, and he started whistling; he had actually pieced together the entire chain of events and thought that he was onto something.

He started by first telling them that the group of East Asians hadn't returned to watch the match but walked straight out of the stadium. Two, they may not have been die-hard football fans, but if they were moving out, why did Mr Trench-coat choose to light up a cigar? Why not before while watching the football match, or why not after leaving the stadium? Most importantly, why did Mr Trench-coat let the cigar slip out of his fingers and then make no attempt to retrieve it?

Sonny added that it appeared that the East Asians were at the stadium not so much to watch the match but to drop the cigar. "And the way they walked out of the stadium after Mr Trench-coat dropped the cigar, there is a strong possibility that they did not want to be in the stadium after dropping the cigar," piped Anita. "Was it possible?" asked Sonny. "That the cigar contained something which would be activated after it was dropped?" Anita said that Sonny's question could be best answered by Mr Trench-Coat himself, and the 'Ice Lilies' would be able to trace him as they had traced Love Li. Sonny, appearing happy and upbeat, requested 'Ice Lilies' to be as precise and thorough with the identity of Mr Trench-Coat as they were with Love Li's. As 'Ice Lilies' got on to the web to trace out Mr Trench-Coat, Sonny and Vidya, without wasting time, started refining the application for the detection and prevention of Coronavirus.

'IceLilies' copied the photograph from the recording, hacked into the passport and visa sections of China, the EU, the US, and Singapore, and used an application to compare the photograph with the passports and visas issued; in about an hour-plus and they had traced out Mr Trench-Coat. Anita sought the duo's attention and then started reading from her notes; "His name is Bao Ching, and he is a Chinese citizen who has been running a Chinese restaurant in Milan, Italy, from 2015 onwards."

"He is one of three hundred and twenty-one thousand Chinese citizens in Italy running businesses and restaurants or working in various industries. They form almost point five percent of the Italian population, and this figure did not include Chinese who had acquired Italian citizenship. Most of the Chinese in Italy were from the Wenzhou province, which is known for its enterprise and industriousness. However, some Han Chinese also worked in Italy, and Bao Ching was one of them. While the locals looked at them as a threat to their jobs, and there had been anti-Chinese protests, the Italian government was indebted to China for shoring up its economy. The Central Bank of China was practically the owner of FIAT, and so was the case with the top five or six Italian companies. In fact, the Chinese companies had invested heavily across the EU." As she was to end her monologue, Anita, with a wry grin, added that all the personal details of Bao Ching and that of his wife and daughter were also with them.

All of them listened to Ania's inputs very carefully. Sonny complimented the 'IceLilies' for their quick work and wondered aloud if they would need to move to Milan to get hold of Bao Ching and question him about the cigar which he let slip from his fingers at 'Game Zero'. Tanya advised Sonny to catch up with the modern world, as today's James Bonds and Sherlock Holmes operated in the cyber realm, where the 'Ice Lilies' were the uncrowned queens.

"Bao Ching will tell us everything on a secured call and he will never come to know of our identity," she added. As Vidya gave her an admiring look, Tanya started laying out the details of the plan to get Bao Ching to narrate the mystery of the slipped-through-fingers cigar to them.

Chapter 8

The Bear Hug

ATP29, a sophisticated and prolific cyber unit closely associated with FSB, is the Kohinoor in the Russian crown of hackers. Also known as Cosy Bear, it had successfully hacked the White House, the US State Department, and many European governments. It had recently been blamed for hacking entities working on the development and testing of Covid-19 vaccines. Both Anita and Tanya had been recruited into ATP29 and were both admired and envied for their hacking abilities. ATP29, unlike traditional intelligence agencies, was decentralised and collaborative at the same time. All personnel working for ATP29 had nano chip implants, which would provide their location to Moscow across the world to get them out of trouble when required and also keep a watch on their movements.

Generally, the 'IceLilies' stayed put in Amsterdam, in their university, as they were either hacking or enjoying weed and sex. So, when their movement to San Siro Stadium and back popped up on the map, the ATP29 head was intrigued and filed away the input in his brain.

Bao Ching, the 'Ice Lilies' found out, was having an affair with a young Chinese waitress working in his restaurant and had fathered a child, who was about two years old. Unbeknownst to Bao, his 18-year-old daughter had appeared in a couple of adult films to support herself. Her handsome but unemployed Italian boyfriend had coaxed her into it. Tanya's plan was to gather evidence of both these scandals, hack into Bao Ching's bank accounts to drain his funds, and then confront him, demanding an explanation for his actions at the San Siro Stadium during 'Game Zero'.

At 17:05 hours, Bao Ching was busy in his restaurant preparing for the evening rush when his mobile rang. He heard a metallic voice in Chinese confirming if it was Bao Ching on the line. Anita had downloaded a language converter software, and she proceeded to spell out the doomsday scenario to Bao Ching along with the damning photographic evidence, which she sent to his email. By the time Anita finished, Bao Ching was sweating profusely. He told her that he was ready to do anything if he could get his money back into his account and secrets about him and his daughter were not made public. Very softly, Anita asked him about the cigar slipping out from his fingers at the San Siro Stadium during 'Game Zero'.

Bao was shell-shocked: for him, it was a matter done with and forgotten, a discomforting memory erased from his brain. He went numb for a while and then thought of brazening it out, but his mind quickly ruled it out. It also ruled out spinning a yarn because of the catastrophic consequences of not telling the truth. He also knew that if he spilt the beans, the long arms of the Chinese internal security, once they came to know that he had squealed, would ruthlessly strangle him and his family. By now, he was drenched in sweat, and Anita realised his predicament. She offered him a way out, telling him that she was aware of the draconian ways of the Chinese government, and after telling her the whole truth, she would make sure that he, along with his wife and daughter, disappeared from Milan and surfaced elsewhere with new identities safe from the clutches of the Chinese Internal Security Service. Bao listened to her silently, and he wavered.

If he spoke, he'd be as good as dead, courtesy the Chinese, and if he didn't, he would be a pauper; his wife would leave him, and his daughter would suffer a loss of face. The escape offer made by Anita presented Bao a chance to live with his family, however slim it appeared, and he took it.

He conveyed his decision to Anita and narrated the mystery of the cigar which slipped between his fingers. He, Bao, was a member of the Chinese Communist Party and was encouraged to move to Italy, which he did about five years ago. There is a system by which every member across the globe is connected to the party and receives propaganda material online periodically. Bao remained in contact with the party as he set up his restaurant in Milan. He was a football fan, having played it in his school days, and the European enthusiasm for the most beautiful game in the world grew on him, too; he started following the Atlanta football team.

Around mid-January, he got a visitor from the Chinese Communist Party who checked up on his well-being, his business, and his commitment to the Communist Party of China and then left. Two days later, he was back and got Bao to speak with Kun Kar who was all charm and built a rapport with Bao in no time. He asked him about his family, his business, and football. Bao was diffident, to begin with, but gained confidence and told Kun Kar about his love for football and his support for the Atlanta club.

Kun Kar asked Bao if he was aware of the Atlanta-Valencia match on 19th February at San Siro Stadium. Bao confirmed that not only was he aware, but he would also be in the San Siro Stadium to support his team.

Dan shifted the conversation to the Coronavirus and explained to Bao how severe the situation in Wuhan had become. He revealed that, through their Russian contacts, they had learned of a plot involving the US, UK, and Italy to trigger an epidemic in China, starting in Wuhan. The goal, Dan said, was to damage China's global rise and isolate it internationally. While there was no concrete evidence, China was determined to seek revenge for the attack on their homeland. Dan told Bao that the top leadership had decided to retaliate in kind, and he asked if Bao was willing to contribute to the cause. Motivated by this, Bao eagerly agreed to support the party and the country in any way he could.

He was told to go to witness the match as part of his group of local Chinese football fans. One day before the match, a cigar would be delivered to him in a case. The cigar would be hollow from the inside, and a glass vial containing Coronavirus would be placed in the hollow. This cigar was to be dropped inside the stadium from a height of a minimum of four feet to initiate a delayed nano fuze mechanism. After the cigar was dropped, the nano fuze would burst open the vial, and the cigar and the Coronavirus would escape into the air, which would be breathed in by most people present in the stadium.

To minimize the risk of infection, Bao needed to leave the stadium within four minutes of the cigar being dropped. He was also instructed to gather a group of local Chinese fans attending the match who would leave with him. This would ensure that the cigar being dropped would not be noticed. At the end of their conversation, Kun Kar told Bao that he had been specially chosen for the important task and that if it was successful, he would be suitably rewarded, probably by meeting with the president himself.

Bao told Anita that everything went off as planned on the 19th of February at the San Siro Stadium, and they were out of the stadium within three minutes of dropping the cigar. He was able to get the whole group out by promising them free beer at his restaurant while they watched the match on TV. It was business as usual for him until the Coronavirus spread uncontrollably, and people started falling ill and dying. The guilt of dropping a biological bomb that caused so many deaths started weighing heavily on him. He overcame the guilt by explaining to himself that it was an act of revenge for the thousands of Chinese who died in Wuhan and slowly erased the whole episode from his memory. The call from Anita was a rude reminder and had turned his life upside down. Anita thanked Bao for being upfront and told him that she would ring him up again in five minutes.

She wanted to discuss Bao's revelation with Sonny and Vidya.

Bao told her that his mobile phone's battery was nearly empty and he would call her from one of his employees' mobiles instead.

The Chinese DCM got Love Li to speak with Dan. Love Li was livid at being betrayed and set up. He confirmed that the airport security personnel knew what they were looking for. Dan asked Love Li to calm down and rethink in case he had told anybody else about his plan. After taking a few deep breaths and reviewing the entire sequence of events since his conversation with Dan, Love Li confirmed that he had not spoken to anyone, nor had he shared or discussed the assassination plan with anyone.

It was then Dan's turn to go into the thinking mode: the plan was known only to Love Li and him. If just the two of them knew the detailed plan, the only way for it to get leaked was for their discussion on WeChat to be listened to. He told Love Li to stop using WeChat and VOIP to communicate sensitive matters and to utilise the embassy's secure communication system. He also had it passed to all his agents and staff to use a secured line of communication for discussing or passing sensitive information. He made a mental note to inform the president and seek his permission to strong-arm the telecommunication company to make WeChat more secure.

After Bao went offline, Anita turned to the other three, who were listening to Bao's confession and asked for their opinion on the authenticity of Bao's narrative. Sonny said that Bao had spoken the truth because he knew that he was caught between the devil and the deep-sea, and his only chance of salvation lay in telling the truth. Vidya and Tanya nodded in agreement, and Vidya asked Anita about Bao's escape plan, but before she could answer him, her mobile phone rang.

Bao was calling from one of his local employees' mobile phones, and this saved him and his family from certain death.

Anita laid out the escape plan for him. He and his family were booked on a flight taking off from Schiphol Airport to Hong Kong five hours from now. They were to move to Schiphol Airport in the next half an hour with only a suitcase each and leaving everything else as it was. Instead of using his car, Bao was to order a taxi for Schiphol Airport and at the border, he was to make sure that their names were not noted down. They were to leave their mobile phones behind and utilise the taxi driver's mobile phone in case of an emergency.

On reaching the airport, their tickets to Hong Kong and new passports and mobiles were to be collected from locker number 19 with its passcode 0835. On reaching Hong Kong, they would be one of the many ethnic

Chinese who could reboot their lives, protected by the anti-Mainland sentiments and respect for individuals and their privacy. In locker number 19, Bao would also find an online password for his new bank account in HSBC Bank, Hong Kong. All the money from his present bank account would be transferred there in the next three hours. All credit cards, debit cards, and driving licences too were to be left behind. It would be a rebirth for the three of them as they landed in Hong Kong. Bao sensed some hope and mumbled a word of thanks. Anita told him that he had no time to lose and should head for the airport immediately.

As Anita instructed Tanya to get to work on the passports, tickets, and bank account, she cheerfully responded that she had already begun working as she overheard her conversation with Bao. She blocked three seats on the flight to Hong Kong, and she was working on the passports, which would be ready in another hour. She requested Anita to work on opening a bank account in Hong Kong and transferring money into it from Bao's bank in Milan. Tanya added that she would make hard copies of the passports, tickets, and the password for the bank account and drive off to Schiphol Airport along with Vidya and place them in locker number 19, which was rented in the name of 'IceLilies'.

Bao's family moved from Milan in a Mercedes taxi within half an hour of Bao's confession. They crossed the border in another one and a half hours, with their faces partially covered by masks; the CCTV cameras recorded them as such.

All the hard copies of the passports, tickets, and passwords were ready in an hour and a half, and Tanya and Vidya drove to Schiphol Airport, opened locker number 19, placed the hard copies inside, and shut it. They were back in their flat before Bao's taxi entered the airport.

All governments like to keep a watch on their citizens, mostly to nip anti-state activities in the bud. In democracies, the right to privacy makes it difficult for the government to monitor its citizens. As a result, there are complex systems in place that require permissions for surveillance.

Communist governments, however, have no such constraints and do so as a matter of course. In China, mobile conversations are screened by software installed on the servers, which flag all suspicious conversations, a system not known to 'Ice Lilies'. Their conversation with Bao was flagged by the software, and since it mentioned Kun Kar's name, it was brought to his attention. He immediately passed it on to Dan and also told him about 'Game Zero'.

The Bao family was half an hour away from Schiphol Airport at that time.

As the Head of the Internal Security Service, Dan had dealt with many crises. After reading the entire conversation, he immediately recognized that he was facing a potential crisis. He needed to figure out who the caller was and how they knew about the cigar and Bao. He asked his Comn Int head to trace the call, identify the caller, and inform him immediately. Next, he called his agent in the Chinese embassy in Italy and instructed him to pick up Bao and his family and interrogate Bao to get all the details of the mysterious caller.

Dan then debated whether to tell the president or not: he wanted to inform him after he had been able to get the identity of the caller, but the potential of the crisis and the stakes involved compelled him to book a call for the president.

It was early morning in Beijing when the president took Dan's call. He listened to him patiently without interrupting. Once Dan had finished, he curtly told him to identify and trace the caller, pick up Bao and his family, and inform him immediately. Dan had been working with the president for a long time, and he realised that the president was unhappy with him. Dan's thoughts were correct. Initially, the president considered replacing him with Kun Kar but ultimately decided to give Dan one more chance. The president believed the case needed to be resolved quickly, as the cigar incident, if it went viral on social media, could turn China into a global pariah.

The president let his mind think through the crisis: Grump was ensuring that their relations kept going southwards. The arrest of Dickson Yeo, a Singaporean Chinese, and his confession that he was spying for China was the latest in the series of Chinese in the US being portrayed as spies. The three US naval aircraft carriers continued to exercise in the South China Sea, and Microsoft was being told to buy out TikTok's US operations.

India was being obdurate about the border standoff in Ladakh. It banned many of the Chinese apps and denied Chinese companies the opportunity to participate in various projects. It also ordered a review of the academic tie-up of the Confucius institute, promoting Chinese language, culture, and education with universities.

Australians were openly criticizing China's rights and policies in the South China Sea, referencing a 2016 ruling by the Permanent Court of Arbitration, which sided with the Philippines against China.

Chinese hackers had also been blamed, along with the Russians and the Iranians, for trying to steal the secret of the Coronavirus vaccine. That brought a smile on Winnie the Pooh's face: why would China be hacking for secrets of the vaccine when WVI R&D section had all the details? The Westerners were trying to pin his country down as the source of the Coronavirus while they were to be blamed for the initial outbreak. 'Game Zero,' he thought to himself, was an example of perfect revenge. From 'Game Zero,' his mind took a cue, and he booked an urgent call for Boot-In, the Russian President. He had provided the inputs regarding western complicity in the virus outbreak at Wuhan and all the help for planning and executing the revenge strikes. He knew that the 'Game Zero' story had to be stopped before it leaked out, and only Boot-In could help.

It was 5 a.m. in Moscow, and Boot-In was still in bed. He took the call and let his annoyance show by a gruff "yes." After apologising for calling at an unearthly hour, Winnie the Pooh told Boot-In all that Dan had narrated and then added that Boot-In's band of hackers, the best in the world, would be able to home in on the mysterious caller and prevent the Game Zero story from leaking out.

Boot-In told Winnie the Pooh not to fret as his hacker warriors would take care of the mysterious caller and told him to get Dan to coordinate the operation with the Commanding Officer of ATP 29.

After hanging up, Winnie the Pooh got Dan online and told him to get cracking on the case in concert with the Commanding Officer of ATP 29. Almost simultaneously, Boot-In called the Commanding Officer ATP 29 and told him to trace the mysterious caller and eliminate him and anyone with whom the information and evidence had been shared. As Boot-In got back into bed, he knew he had successfully trapped "Winnie the Pooh" and planned to undermine him at just the right moment. The memory of the USSR's breakup and China's role in it haunted him daily, fueling his determination to restore Russia's lost glory.

Sonny briefly texted the inputs given by Bao to his three colleagues, and now the story of 'Game Zero' was known to six people, not counting the Chinese and the Russians.

THREE GORGES AND ROOF OF THE WORLD

Three Gorges Dam is the biggest hydroelectric dam in the world, with an installed capacity of 22,500 MW. It was dreamt of by Chang Kai Shek. Its construction started in 1994, and it became functional in 2018. It is built across the span of the Yangtze River, the third longest river in the world, which begins its journey from the Tanggula Mountains in the Tibetan plateau and flows approximately 6300 kilometres eastwards into the East China Sea near the city of Shanghai. The city of Wuhan is on the banks of the Yangtze River, and its fate is tied to both the Three Gorges Dam and the Yangtze River.

Floods are an annual occurrence in the Yangtze River, and the three Gorges Dam controls the water outflow to prevent Wuhan's flooding. In rare cases, The Three Gorges Dam is forced to release water to prevent the dam from overflowing.

The Yangtze River was in full spate when Husn and Aashiq reached Wuhan, and though the excess water in the Three Gorges Dam was being released in a controlled fashion, in another two hours, it would start flooding the streets of Wuhan. The citizens of Wuhan had been warned to stay indoors. It was also reported by a TV news channel that the flooding of Wuhan was being carried out intentionally by the Chinese government to thwart the investigation of the WHO team scheduled to visit Wuhan.

Interestingly, the mandate of the team was to determine how the zoonotic Coronavirus was transmitted to humans.

As Husn and Aashiq came down to the lobby, the director, WVI, called Husn, informed her about the flooding of a few stretches in Wuhan and suggested that they visit the institute the next morning.

Aashiq had already checked on the flooding and had told Husn that they would be able to make it to the institute and back as scheduled. Husn politely conveyed that they would like to stick to the original schedule.

The director, though still slightly apprehensive, said that he would wait for them in his office. The bat woman who was waiting in the lobby didn't have any such misgivings. She asked them to get into her 2008 Mitsubishi Pajero, and they drove off towards WVI. Some of the streets were flooded, but the Pajero drove through imperiously, and soon they were on the hilly road to WVI, which was bone dry, and they made it in good time. As they branched off for the institute, Aashiq noticed a nondescript car following in their wake. He had noticed it struggling behind them on the flooded streets, too. With the traffic practically non-existent, he became suspicious and brain texted his suspicions. Husn, who was in conversation with the bat woman, checked in the sideview mirror, noticed the car, and brain texted that it was most likely the Internal Security Service monitoring their movements.

They were at the gates of WVI in about seventy-five minutes because of the slow going initially. At the gate, they were asked to take off their clothes and shoes and were given dungarees and slippers to wear. After they changed, they were required to pass through an X-ray screening cubicle, confirming they were clear and permitted to enter the institute. The bat woman left her car in the parking lot, then transported the duo to the main office in a battery-operated golf cart.

As they entered the office complex, Husn noticed that the whole place was quiet and desolate. Suddenly, from the side corridor, a young scientist wearing a full protective personnel suit walked into Aashiq, who was walking behind the bat woman and Husn. They both fell, and the scientist was very apologetic as he helped Aashiq get up. The bat woman laughed as he saw both sprawled on the ground. She introduced the scientist as Waxin Li and said that he was one of their most brilliant, but he was so lost that he could walk into a wall without noticing it!

Both Husn and Aashiq expressed their pleasure at meeting Waxin Li, who was in a state of embarrassed discomfiture and begged their leave at the first opportune moment.

Another minute and they were in the director's office, who received them warmly and offered them green tea. As the tea was being served, Aashiq requested directions to the nearest restroom. The restroom was at the other end of the corridor, and as Aashiq walked to it, his right hand slipped into the pant pocket, and he checked the piece of paper that Waxin Li had thrust into his hand while helping him get up. As Aashiq entered the restroom, he noticed CCTV cameras, so he kept looking down as he peed and read the cryptic note written on that small piece of paper. The note, written in Urdu, instructed them to request a visit to the Research and Development wing and to meet him in cabin number 6. There, Waxin Li would discreetly hand them a small vial sealed within a snake's venom sac. It was to be placed between the tongue and lower molar and taken back by them to the hotel. The note ended abruptly after conveying that Waxin Li would have dinner with them at the hotel. As Aashiq zipped up, he brain texted the message.

They were waiting for him, and as Aashiq returned, the director told them that his number two, the world-famous bat woman, would be with them throughout the audit.

As they got up from their chairs, Husn asked the director if they could start the audit from the Research and Development section. Both the director and the bat woman were surprised, and the bat woman quickly retorted that the audit should commence from the basic sections to the R&D section. It would be better if the audit could commence the next day as the institute would shut in a couple of hours.

Husn, giving an endearing smile to the director, said that she had heard so much about the R&D section and pleaded that they be allowed to visit it today to just look around. She added that they would commence the audit the next day in the manner suggested by the bat woman. Again, it was the bat woman who spoke: she told the director that Husn's plea could be agreed to, and she would personally conduct the duo through the R&D section. Actually, the bat woman wanted the audit to start well and was confident that she could handle the duo's visit to the R&D section. After all, she thought, it was just a visit and she would be able to herd them through in quick time.

The director gave them his go-ahead, and bat woman asked for the golf cart to take them to the R&D section. As they waited for the golf cart, doubts clouded Husn's mind, and she brain texted Aashiq, asking him if it was the right decision to visit the R&D section based on a note from an unknown person. Could it be a trap that they were walking into?

Aashiq replied that if it was a trap, they could explain it all by saying that they were curious to know the truth and they would hand over the vial to the bat woman if it was in their possession. Husn wasn't fully convinced by Aashiq's explanation but decided to play along.

The duo had to utilise their thumbs and eye retinas to gain entry into the R&D section and had to put on suits, similar to what Waxin Li was wearing when he had rammed into Aashiq.

As they entered the main area of the laboratory, they were impressed with its vast and immaculate layout. It was a hub-and-spokes design with a large circular area serving as an informal, casual area with various indoor games placed on tables, coffee and tea vending machines, TV screens, and yoga mats. Bat woman explained that the scientists working in the section had individual cabins to work in, and the central area was designed to provide them with all amenities to help them de-stress and recharge their creative juices.

The duo noticed two of the scientists hunched over the chessboard, four of them playing pool, and the rest, unmindful of the visitors, engrossed in computer games. Bat woman was planning to get the duo to meet a couple of scientists, show them their cabins, and return to the hotel in good time.

Suddenly, a scientist emerged from one of the spokes, walking at a very fast pace, and all the other scientists lounging around the common area gave him a wide berth! As he shot past, bat woman recognised Waxin Li and hoped he reached his destination without an accident. However, much to her dismay, Waxin Li came to an abrupt halt, about-turned, walked back to her and asked her the reason for being in the common area. Bat woman told him that the duo, whom he had already met, were keen to visit the R&D section, and she was showing them around. Waxin Li immediately offered to take them to his cabin, but bat woman told him not to bother and to get on with whatever he was planning to do, moving with such alacrity!

Bat woman knew that Waxin Li had already researched a vaccine for Coronavirus, and she didn't want this information to be leaked out by any chance.

She had also promised her pharma benefactors not to let the duo anywhere near the vaccine.

In response to bat woman's stern refusal of his offer, Waxin Li was at his voluble best and, in a comic but pleasant way, almost forced them towards cabin number six. Once there, he started talking a dime a dozen, and Husn was having a tough time translating Waxin's Mandarin into English for Aashiq. She realised that she had had enough and said that she wanted to return to the hotel.

Bat woman, who was on her toes to ensure that Waxin Li, in his exuberance, didn't let out anything about the vaccine, used Husn's request to excuse themselves and head out of Waxin Li's cabin. Waxin appeared disappointed but bowed gallantly to both the ladies and shook Aashiq's hand. Realising that Waxin had placed a piece of paper along with something else in his hand, Aashiq quickly placed both items in his pocket and turned to get out of the cabin. Bat woman got them out of the R&D section and took them straight to the institute's entry/exit gate. During the short journey to the gate, Aashiq, taking advantage of sitting alone in the rear seat, took out the piece of paper and the other item, which indeed was a vial, and placed them both in his mouth as instructed. At the gate, they were again x-rayed, changed their dress, and got into the Pajero.

Husn sat in the front seat with bat woman, and Aashiq got into the rear seat behind the driver's seat. There was very light traffic, and they moved fast on the hilly section of the road. Husn again noticed a car tailing them, though it maintained a good distance from the Pajero. As bat woman and Husn chatted away in Mandarin, Aashiq was engrossed in his mobile; he was actually trying to read the note that Wasim Li had thrust into his hand in his cabin.

The note was in Urdu, and after a while, Aashiq's eyes got used to the dim light and the movement of the car. The note read, "You know me as Waxin Li, but I was born as Taj Mohamad to a pious Muslim couple in Kashgar, a historic city in Xinjiang province. At the age of three, my name was changed to Taj Zakhir because words like Mohammad and Islam were banned by the Chinese government.

We are peace-loving Turkic Uighur Muslims who have settled in Xinjiang province for centuries. Xinjiang became a part of China only in 1949 after the Communist Government came into power, and it is important to China because of its oil and natural gas deposits and the Belt and Road Initiative, which is planned through it. Uneasy with the locals' religious beliefs, the Communist Government, in 2001/2002, set a plan in motion to settle Han Chinese in the province and prevent us from following Islam.

People have been arrested and kept in concentration camps & some of them have just disappeared. Religious persecution has only increased over the years, and in 2019, the UN, USA, and the European Union voiced their concern over it. Surprisingly, Turkey was the only

Islamic country to voice its concern, while other Islamic countries like Saudi Arabia and Pakistan praised China for the actions it had taken.

He, Taj Zakhir, blessed with a very high IQ, was picked up by the Chinese government, educated in Beijing, and his skills were exploited in the field of research. His name was changed again to Waxin Li this time, and he was permitted to meet his parents in Kashgar only once in three years while studying in Beijing. Outwardly, I, Waxin Li, am now a thoroughbred Chinese, but inside me burns an intense fire of revenge fanned further by every despicable act committed by the Chinese Communist government against the Uighur Muslims.

The R&D section of the WVI develops new virus'and their vaccine, too. I helped develop both the Coronavirus and its vaccine. And it was me who injected some bats with Coronavirus and let them be sold in the Wuhan wet market to avenge the killing and torture of my fellow Uighurs by the Han Chinese. The vial that I have given you contains the vaccine for Coronavirus.

I have my sources, and I was told about your visit and also that you are a fellow Muslim and Husn, a Tibetan, who is acutely pained by the illegal occupation of Tibet and brutal suppression of the Tibetans. I am confident that you would be able to smuggle the vaccine out of the institute and put it in the right hands.

While I have been able to avoid any suspicion of my involvement in the spread of zoonotic Coronavirus,

I know that the Chinese will sooner or later cotton on and come after me. Therefore, I have an escape plan ready.

You will receive two sets of steward uniforms along with the room service trolley. The Chief Steward of Shangri La Hotel, a fellow Uighur, is arranging it. Change into the uniforms and meet me at the staff entrance of the hotel sharp at 22:00 hours tonight."

Aashiq let it all sink in and then texted the whole message to Husn and sought her opinion. A few minutes later, Husn responded, saying that Waxin seemed trustworthy and that they would follow his plan.

Their journey back to the hotel took less than an hour, and as the bat woman left them in the lobby, both of them confirmed room service for dinner. As they stood in the lobby, Husn, with her back to the main entrance, was watching out to confirm her suspicions of being followed in the huge mirror placed behind the receptionist. She noticed the Li sisters come in with a gap of about a minute and then move to different seating areas in the lobby, keeping a wary eye on Aashiq and her. Seeing them in the lobby, her photographic memory conveyed that they were the pretty air hostesses on their flight to Beijing whose expressions had suddenly become dour. She was happy with her memory but alarmed at the prospect of being followed, especially after reading Aashiq's latest brain text.

She immediately brain texted Aashiq, who located the Li sisters through the corner of his eyes and replied they had to be wary of the unwanted company, She quickly brain-texted Aashiq, who discreetly spotted the Li sisters and responded that they should stay alert despite the sisters' charm. They took the elevator to their floor, agreed to have dinner in their own rooms, and planned to be in bed by 21:15.

Back at the WVI the Chief of Security, Senior Colonel Peng Ma, was going through the CCTV footage of the daily activities at the institute. A veteran of the Intelligence Corps, he was more a cloak-and-dagger man and followed two dictums, 'Suspect all' and 'there is more to it than meets the eye'. As he worked through the footage, his eyes were missing nothing, and he also noticed Waxin Li initially colliding with Aashiq and then taking the duo to his cabin.

He was aware of the purpose of the duo's visit and so decided to watch both videos in slow motion but could not pick up anything suspicious. He told himself that it was all normal as nothing showed up in the footage, and Waxin Li was known to be barging into people, lost in his thoughts.

Finally Senior Colonel PengMa decided to call it a day and drove off after the mandatory security check. He hummed as he drove and on an impulse dialled bat woman to ask her about the duo's visit. Bat woman told him that it was all routine except for the maverick Waxin Li barging into them twice.

Peng Ma thanked her and disconnected. He was now suspicious because Waxin Li accidentally bumping into them twice was too much of a coincidence. He decided to go by Shangri La Hotel to check on Husn and Aashiq. His eyes glanced at the dashboard clock: it was 21:15 hours. His ETA at the hotel, he calculated, was 22:00 hours.

Li sisters moved into their rooms and kept a watch on Husn and Aashiq through the cameras. They watched the dinner trolley coming into Husn and Aashiq's rooms, and dinner was served by the same waiter. In both rooms, a tray with a water jug and glass tumbler was placed on the sideboard by the waiter; the dress was neatly taped under the tray. Both Husn and Aashiq had their dinner, were in bed by 21:15 hours and were sound asleep by 21:30 hours.

Though the Li sisters were still in surveillance mode, their focus was reduced as they watched their prey get into their respective beds and the lights being switched off. Anne moved to her sister's room to have dinner together, and both took their eyes off the cameras as they discussed what to order. In all this, they missed out on Husn and Aashiq getting up and changing into stewards' uniforms.

At 21:45 hours, Li's sisters noticed the dinner trolley being moved out of the rooms occupied by Husn and Aashiq. As they appreciated the prompt clearance of the plates and bowls and looked forward to their own dinner, they failed to notice Husn and Aashiq crawl out of their rooms, screened by the trolley and the waiter.

Once out of the rooms, the duo moved to the staff entrance, through the main dining restaurant and the kitchen. No one gave a second glance as they moved in a measured hurry, avoiding eye contact and appearing totally focused on the task at hand.

At 22:00 hours, as senior Colonel Peng Ma was received in the lobby by the security manager, Waxin Li, dressed in a black tracksuit, met Husn and Aashiq at the staff entrance of the hotel.

Senior Colonel Peng Ma requested the security manager to provide the CCTV footage of the duo's arrival and stay at the hotel. The footage was provided promptly without any questions, and as Peng Ma viewed it in fast-forward mode, he spotted two additional stewards coming out of the duo's rooms at 21:45 hours and entering the service lift. He realised that something was amiss and decided to check both Aashiq and Husn's rooms. The sense of urgency was evident as he got the master keys collected from the reception and rushed to the rooms, only to find that the birds had flown the coop.

The switching on of lights in the rooms also alerted the Li sisters.

Peng Ma's mind raced as he called up Waxin Li to connect the dots, but his phone did not respond; Peng Ma's suspicion was confirmed. Next, Peng Ma called up the Director to inform him that the trio of Waxin Li, Husn, and Aashiq had gone missing, and he was going to report the matter to the local police.

The director, who knew more about Waxin Li's work than Peng Ma, rushed to WVI along with the bat woman.

Anne Li rang up the 'number two' in Beijing and informed that the duo had escaped from the hotel. This input was given to Dan at the very next moment.

Director and the bat woman reached the institute in forty-five minutes and rushed to cabin number six. On checking, their worst fears were confirmed: the vial containing the vaccine was missing and all the associated information on Waxin Li's desktop, related to the vaccine, had been deleted. In panic, the director called up Kun Kar.

Winnie the Pooh received calls from Kun Kar & Dan within minutes of each other and blew his top. He got both of them on a conference call and told them in a menacing and cold tone that he wanted the heads of the trio served to him on a platter as soon as possible, or else a couple of heads would definitely roll in Beijing.

Both Kun Kar and Dan felt a shiver go down their spine. Dan ordered checks on all exit roads, Wuhan airport, and the railway station, put his 'A' team to track the trio electronically, and ordered the local police to start a massive physical search in Wuhan. At 01:00 hours, he flew out to Wuhan in a Lear jet and landed at 02:45 hours.

Kun Kar followed him in the morning, and they both met at the Shangri La Hotel at 09:00 hours the next day.

Chapter 9

Football, Flowers, and the Indian Rope Trick

The Commanding Officer of ATP 129 had received a call from Dan a few minutes after President Boot-In's instruction. Dan told him that the transcript of the entire conversation between Bao and the unknown caller had been sent to ATP 129. Bao and the family had just upped and left, leaving everything behind. However, they had been spotted at the Italy-Holland border in a Mercedes taxi, which had been tracked to Schiphol Airport. The caller remained unidentified, as a software had been used to alter the voice, conceal the phone number and location details.

The Commanding Officer got hold of the transcript and read it very deliberately. As he finished reading it, he realised that the whole operation was the handiwork of persons highly skilled in hacking and decided to put a thief to catch a thief. He picked up his mobile and dialled Anita's number to put 'IceLilies' on the job but cut the call as he remembered that both Anita and Tanya had visited the San Siro Stadium recently. Next, he asked his communication surveillance wing to provide him with the call data records of Anita and Tanya for the last forty-eight hours. The details were emailed to him a few minutes later, and he quickly reviewed them. Both individuals had made only four or five routine calls, and neither phone record showed any calls during the time Anita spoke with Bao.

CO 129 ATP overlooked checking out VOIP, which would have told him that a call was made by Anita at the same time when the unknown caller forced Bao to confess.

Partially satisfied with these checks, CO 129 called up Anita. She had seen his earlier missed call and was on her guard as she answered.

Her Commanding Officer came straight to the point and told her to find out the whereabouts of the mysterious caller and inform him immediately. He asked her to get all the details of the call from the communication surveillance wing, and, as he was about to disconnect, he asked her about the 'IceLilies' visit to the San Siro Stadium.

Anita was stumped by his question but, regaining her composure, replied that both she and Tanya were fans of the Atlanta football club team and wanted to experience the majestic stadium and its museum, especially because the club had won its last match there. "That's nice," said her CO, "I didn't know that both of you were Atlanta fans. I'm sure you must be disappointed with them now."

Anita was at a loss for words. She had no knowledge of Atlanta's performance post 'Game Zero'. Requesting her CO to repeat his question as she couldn't hear him properly, she snatched Tanya's phone and googled the club's latest performance details.

But before she could get any further in her search, he informed her in a soft but ominous tone that Atlanta football club had been beaten by Paris Saint-Germain (PSG) football club 2-1 in the UEFA Champions League Quarterfinal match just the day before, and he hung up.

Anita was transfixed as the three of them looked askance at her. Finally, Sonny broke the silence and asked her why she appeared shell-shocked.

CO ATP 129 believed that in the profession of global espionage, everyone was guilty until proven innocent. He was certain that Anita had lied to him. She was no fan of Atlanta FC or else she would have definitely known the result of the quarter final match played two days earlier. He decided to have the 'IceLilies' picked up for questioning and dialled the DCM at the Russian embassy in Holland.

Anita repeated the conversation with her CO verbatim to Tanya, Sonny, & Vidya and added that it was more the ominous tone that the CO used to convey that she was lying, which was worrisome. Sonny tried to assuage her feelings, saying that she was reading more into the tone than necessary and that the situation wasn't so bad. Tanya told Sonny that the Russians were different; CO ATP 129 already knew about the mysterious caller, their visit to San Siro Stadium and Anita's lie about her love for Atlanta FC.

He would by now be arranging to pick up the 'Ice Lilies' for interrogation. Vidya was listening to all this time, and he suggested that there was no need to panic presently; however, it would be prudent to vacate their apartment immediately and plan ahead while keeping the apartment under watch. All of them agreed and, within minutes, were out of the apartment and into the nearby park from where they could keep an unobtrusive watch on the apartment. Fifteen minutes later, two men drove up to the apartment in a car bearing Russian embassy number plates. The driver was big and burly, whereas the other person was short and stocky. Finding the apartment locked, the big and burly Russian pushed hard at the door with his shoulder and broke into the apartment.

'IceLilies', Sonny and Vidya witnessed them breaking into the apartment, were convinced of their evil intentions, and hot-footed to a nondescript café in the Centraal. Once there, Sonny called up the CIA station Chief and sought his help as he narrated their unenviable situation while confirming that Husn and Aashiq were also on the run.

Station Chief asked him if the 'IceLilies' were carrying their mobiles, to which Sonny replied in the affirmative. The Station Chief told Sonny that the 'IceLilies' should take the sims out of their mobiles and throw them in the canal.

'IceLilies' also needed to be searched thoroughly, the Station chief said, for any chips implanted in their bodies. He told them to destroy all the chips found implanted and then meet him at their previous Rendezvous (RV). Following the station chief's instructions, the nano-chips implanted on the inside of the right wrist of 'IceLilies' were detected and destroyed, their mobile SIM cards thrown in the canal, and the four of them moved swiftly on foot to the RV.

Once inside the apartment, the two Russians conducted a thorough search for the 'IceLilies.' They didn't find them but realized the apartment had been hastily abandoned. They also discovered that the 'IceLilies' had two male guests: Sonny and Vidya. The short and stocky Russian called CO ATP 129 and gave him all the inputs. CO ATP 129 found out 'IceLilies' locations through the implanted chips, provided it to his team and ordered the elimination of all four of them. Next, he updated Boot In through a secure email and waited impassively as he monitored his team's progress. He smiled as he thought of 'IceLilies' in the past tense. He was too hard-boiled a professional to feel any remorse or regret; they signed their own death warrant.

His team was minutes away from the café when Dan called him from Wuhan and told him about Love Li and offered his services as he was in Amsterdam itself.

CO ATP 129 just grunted in response and informed Dan about 'Ice Lilies' ' & their male friends' elimination in the next ten to fifteen minutes. He also gave Dan the names of the two male friends. Dan took but a second to realise that Sonny and Vidya had fooled them and not returned to the US.

He narrated the whole story to the CO ATP 129, who laughed and said that his team would complete Love Li's job for him!

Sonny pinged the CIA Station Chief after they reached the RV. The Station Chief sent a message, informing them that he was waiting 500 meters ahead in a second-hand Volkswagen Beetle. He instructed them to approach him one at a time, two minutes apart, keeping their heads down to avoid being detected by CCTV cameras.

Station Chief had realised that last time, Love Li had made use of the CCTV cameras covering the streets to spot and follow them all the way to the US Embassy.

Once all four of them had huddled into the rather small car, he drove them to a friend's apartment who was in California on a business visit. He planned to call up his Director after leaving them in the apartment. He was sure that his Director would order their immediate evacuation to the US and, therefore, did not move them to the embassy. He also knew that a US Air Force aircraft was parked at Schiphol Airport, which could be used to fly the four out without any delay.

Chapter 10

The End Game

The Russian team reached the café and found it nearly empty, with no sign of their targets. As one of them ordered coffee, his partner checked the restroom and the kitchen in case they were hiding there. He returned to the table and told his partner that his search had been in vain. As the waiter brought their coffees, the senior of the two nonchalantly inquired about four friends of theirs, two Russian girls and two men, an American and an Indian. The café did not get too many customers, so the waiter clearly remembered that four people who matched the description had come to the café earlier and had left about fifteen minutes earlier.

CO ATP 129 was informed immediately and requested the new location of 'IceLilies'. He could not get their locations as the chips had been extracted from their bodies and thrown into the canal. He smiled again because he liked a good chase and got Dan to put Love Li on their tail.

Love Li was on standby and wasted no time tracking the four of them to the RV. Instructing the Russian team to move there as CO ATP 129 listened in, he started looking for the CIA station chief in the area of the RV but met with no success initially as he couldn't spot the station chief's car. He then started looking at the faces of the drivers and was able to home in on the Volkswagen Beetle. He also spotted the 'Ice Lilies' along with Sonny and Vidya as they each got into the Volkswagen Beetle separately. A minute after they were all inside, the car drove away.

Love Li had expected the car to head toward the U.S. Embassy, but instead, it turned toward the city center and entered Dam Square. The square was crowded, and he quickly lost sight of the Volkswagen Beetle as it moved into an area shielded from CCTV cameras. Unable to track it due to the numerous similar cars, he directed the kill team to relocate to Dam Square.

CO ATP 129 decided to update Boot In because of the involvement of the CIA station chief. He didn't want the Americans to step in and save the troublesome four lest the truth of 'Game Zero' got out. The mystery of the slippery cigar had to be buried along with the troublesome four.

Boot-In wasn't happy to know that the troublesome four were still at large and, worse, were being helped by the CIA station chief. He also didn't want the 'Game Zero' story to gain any traction because of its potential to cause irreparable and long-term damage. He told CO 129 to redouble his efforts, cut the call and dialled a number.

A Russian mole, who also had hacking skills had been planted in the White House which was only known by a handler and Boot In. Following Boot In's instructions, the mole leaked an email framing Sonny and Vidya as Russian spies working with the 'Ice Lilies'. The email falsely claimed they were planning a cyber-attack on key U.S. installations to incite racial riots. It also hinted they would soon be entering the U.S. with the assistance of the Station Chief in Amsterdam. The CIA took the bait completely, and the Director requested Grump's permission to detain them. Relying on this information, Grump approved. The mole then confirmed to Boot In that the Americans had fallen for the setup.

The Director called up the Station Chief next and briefed him about the leaked email and Grump's permission to bring them in. The Station Chief had his reservations about the complicity of Sonny and Vidya and conveyed it to his Director. He also conveyed that they were in touch with him, and currently, they were at one of his friend's places in Amsterdam itself. "Good," said the Director, "put all of them on a USAF aircraft the next morning bound for Washington." The Station Chief, confident that the email was the handiwork of the Russians and that they, the troublesome four, would prove to be the fabulous four to the agency with their inputs, agreed. The leaked email also popped up on 'Ice Lilies' laptops because it mentioned their names: an algorithm they had configured ensured that.

The email came as a shocker, and Tanya also got the details of the conversation between the Director and the Station Chief. Sonny was most upset because the Americans had, without any verification, decided to arrest them. Vidya told him to look beyond the betrayal and suggested that they avoid being taken to the US. As all of them nodded in agreement, he could only think of Paddy and called him on VOIP to suggest a way out. After listening to Vidya, Paddy put him through to Kala Brahmin (KB) immediately; Paddy and KB were old friends, and he knew that if anyone could help the four escape, it was KB because he was a daredevil former Intelligence Bureau officer who was currently India's NSA.

Vidya called KB using the number provided by Paddy and introduced himself. KB was expecting the call as he had already received Paddy's message. He instructed Vidya to disconnect and call him back from a secure line. Vidya then shared details about Game Zero, the vaccine, and the betrayal. KB listened quietly, and after a long pause, he told Vidya to head to Brussels airport as soon as possible. There, he would arrange for their escape to India on the Vande Bharat Air India flight, which was bringing back travellers stranded due to the Coronavirus. Immediately after reaching the airport, Vidya was to send his location to KB.

Before Vidya could google for the possible, safest, and fastest routes to Brussels airport, Anita suggested that they reach the trucker station on Risjenhout A4, about twenty minutes away, and get into one of the trucks taking flowers to Brussels airport for export. She added that it would be safer than taking a taxi to Brussels airport.

Without wasting time, the four of them trooped out to take a taxi to Risjenhout A4. As they were getting out of the house, Vidya suggested that they take separate taxis to Risjenhout and meet up at the trucker station on the A4 highway there. He also cautioned about the CCTV cameras and suggested covering their faces. Ice Lilies and Sonny nodded in agreement, put on their face masks, and moved off singly, in shadows, to board their respective taxis.

Love Li had finally been able to spot the Volkswagen Beetle and tracked it to the house where the Gang of Four was hiding. He noticed the CIA station chief driving out alone in his Volkswagen Beetle, and his adrenaline started pumping as he sensed the location of his prey. Asking the two Russians to get into his car, he mapped out the route in his mind: their destination was about twenty minutes away.

He stopped the car about two hundred metres from the house, and the three of them jogged up silently to find the entrance door ajar. Asking the Russians to cover the entry & exit of the house, Love Li climbed up to the first-floor with practised ease and entered through the attic. As he started his search, he sensed the house was empty. Nevertheless, he, along with the two Russians, searched the house thoroughly, only to confirm what he had suspected: the Gang of Four had escaped again. Love Li decided to fall back on the CCTVs to spot and track their prey.

Sonny–Vidya and the Ice Lilies had left just ten minutes earlier. Ironically, it was the leaked email that saved them from certain death.

The last of the four, Vidya, reached the Rendezvous forty-five minutes after leaving the house, and they got into a huddle to chalk out their further course of action.

Initially, the majority view was to get into the trailer unseen and hide themselves in the stacks of flowers, but Vidya disagreed. He said that getting into the body of the truck would entail opening the rear doors, which, like all other doors, would be electronically operated and that they did not have the luxury of time. Otherwise, IceLilies would have hacked into the truck's operating system and got them a free ride. As Tanya nodded appreciatively, Vidya suggested that instead of their hacking skills, the Ice Lilies use their persuasive powers to help them hitch a lift. Tanya smiled and said that the physical charms of 'IceLilies' were as effective as their hacking skills.

Telling them to wait in the shadows of the trailers, she entered the restaurant where most of the truckers were sipping coffee and munching on their ham sandwiches. As the door closed behind her, Tanya looked around until her eyes fell on a driver who appeared to be East European. He was big-built with long blond hair and a scraggy beard. Sonia walked up to him and asked if he understood Russian. As he replied, "Da," Tanya asked him if he was driving his trailer to the Brussels airport. On hearing a 'da' again, Tanya told him that she and her three friends needed to get to the Brussels airport undetected, and he would be paid one thousand Euros for the favour. Looking at Tanya with narrowed eyes, he thought for a while, nodded, and asked her to get her friends to his trailer.

As he paid his bill, Tanya moved out of the restaurant and met up with the rest of them. In five minutes, they reached the designated trailer and met Mr Beard, who asked them to get into the rear of the driver's cabin, confirming that there was no checking at the border and the CCTV cameras would not be able to pick up their masked faces. They climbed into the rear of the driver's cabin, and the trailer moved out of the parking area. It would be at Brussels airport in the next four hours, a distance of about two hundred and thirty kilometres. As Tanya chatted with Mr Beard, he confirmed that the trailer would move to the airside of Brussels airport through gate number 17. Vidya messaged the gate number to KB.

Love Li and the two Russians started scrutinising the CCTV footage within thirty minutes of their finding the house empty. They hoped to detect their prey quickly enough to track and eliminate them, but Vidya's strategy of moving singly, in shadows, and with face masks made detection quite improbable. Initially, they looked for two guys and two girls escaping together, and after an hour of futile scrutiny, they decided to look for two guys and two girls or a combination of moving separately, but again, they met with failure. As time passed, frustration built up, and the three of them got hot under their collars and started blaming each other. Love Li, impassive as ever, was about to ask the other two to cool off when a brainwave struck him, and he told the two Russians to look for their prey moving singly.

Scrutiny of the CCTV footage recommenced with renewed vigour, and they could detect and track the four to A4, Risjenhout, however, by that time, nearly three hours had passed since they began examining the footage. It would take them another half an hour to reach the truckers' station and start inquiring about the 'Gang of Four'.

Love Li was able to sweet-talk the restaurant owner into showing them the CCTV footage and homed on Tanya and Mr Beard. The restaurant owner told Love Li that Mr. Beard was a regular at the restaurant and transported flowers to Brussels airport in the summer months. The short and stocky Russian downloaded the video clip and forwarded it to the Commanding Officer of ATP 129, requesting quick identification of Mr. Beard.

Going by the time recorded on the video clip, Love Li calculated that the trailer would be reaching Brussels airport. He sent the photos of Sonny, Vidya, and 'Ice Lilies' to Dan, requesting their detention at the airport before they boarded a flight and escaped. Dan, badly caught up himself, sent the photographs to the Chinese ambassador in Brussels with instructions to find and detain them before they boarded a flight out of Brussels.

The European Union as a whole had issues with China, but for individual countries, Chinese investments were critical to their economy. The Chinese ambassador's request elicited a positive and quick response, and the airport security personnel started looking out for the four fugitives.

Fifteen minutes earlier, the trailer driven by Mr. Beard had rolled into the airside of the Brussels airport, entering from gate number seventeen. At the gate, Mr. Beard showed the necessary documents, and he waved in without a second glance: he was plying his trade fifteen days a month and was a known face. Five hundred metres from gate number seventeen, Mr Beard asked the passengers in the rear seat to duck and remain so until he entered the airport. On his way to the designated aircraft, Mr Beard dropped them off at an isolated spot after Tanya had transferred one thousand Euros into his bank account. "So far, so good," said Vidya, "let's hope we are contacted before Love Li or the Russians get us."

Rai, also known as Ray to his colleagues and friends in the West, was the Captain of the Dreamliner aircraft being utilised for the Vande Bharat flight ferrying stranded passengers to India. He had been directly contacted by KB, who requested that he evacuate Sonny, Vidya, and 'Ice Lilies'. Rai knew that it was an illegal request and that a slip or leak would put his career in jeopardy. He also knew that he had the right to refuse the request and it was the best option for him. But he did not, rather did not want to refuse; having qualified to study in a prestigious military school as a young boy, he had joined the Indian Air Force as a fighter pilot and wore his patriotism on his sleeve. For personal reasons, he resigned from the Indian Air Force and joined Air India.

After years of flying, he was looking forward to his retirement, but the love for his motherland hadn't dimmed, and KB, who knew about Rai, exploited it, the wily old fox!

Once Rai said yes to the request, he was provided with all the inputs regarding the ETA and airside entry of the four passengers by KB as soon as he received it from Vidya. As he came to know that the trailer would be entering from gate number 17, Rai sweet-talked the local Air India staff into providing him a vehicle and a pair of night binoculars and then chose a suitable spot to keep gate number seventeen under surveillance.

He followed each trailer as it entered and moved to the cargo bay. Fortunately for Rai, the trailer traffic was not very heavy, and he could follow each trailer that entered right up to the cargo bay. Mr Beard's was the eleventh trailer, since Rai had started his surveillance, to enter the airport. Ray tracked the vehicle with his powerful night binoculars, saw it come to a stop, and observed four passengers getting out and gathering in a huddle.

Rai smiled as he counted four of them, got off his surveillance post and got into the car to pick them up. He drove up to them and, introducing himself, asked them to get into the car. Sonny and 'Ice Lilies' looked at Vidya, who gave an imperceptible nod. They climbed into the car with Vidya in the co-driver's seat and the rest in the rear.

Driving well within the laid-down speed limit of forty kilometres per hour, Rai took five minutes to reach his aircraft. Asking them to wait in the car, he used the emergency step ladder next to the aerobridge to board the aircraft. Once on board, he explained the whole situation to the senior flight attendant, Mrs Rita Devi, from Manipur. He had known her for years and was sure that she would come up with a solution. Rita asked Capt. Rai to go down to the car and get the four up the ladder after five minutes.

Meanwhile, she instructed the ground crew to check the boarding passes while she moved some heavy items and asked her junior to assist. As Captain Rai came up along with the four, Rita was at the entry gate of the aircraft and guided them to the seats in the rear as Capt Rai moved into the cockpit. Thirty minutes later, the aircraft took off for New Delhi, and an hour later, three of them were gorging on chicken curry and rice while Vidya was enjoying sambar and rice.

Love Li and the two Russians were trying to contact Mr. Beard as they drove, fast and furious, to Brussels airport. After dropping his consignment at the airport, Mr Beard went to his favourite café at the nearby truck station and checked his mobile as he sipped his beer. He noticed several calls from an unknown number and called it. The senior of the two Russian agents spoke with him and asked about the four passengers whom he had given a lift up to the airport. Mr Beard could sense the underlying threat in the cold tone and thought it better to give out all the details right from Tanya meeting him to his dropping them off at the airport.

CO ATP 129 was informed immediately, and he used his connections in Brussels to spot them through CCTVs covering the airside and their boarding the Vande Bharat flight aided by Capt Rai. By the time he could piece all the information together, the flight was already two hours in the air. He thought for a moment whether to disturb Boot In as it was 02:00 hours in Moscow, decided that the matter was urgent, and called him on a secure line. After hearing CO ATP 129 out, Boot In, still groggy from his evening vodka, was furious at the chicanery of the Indians, and he wanted Russian fighter jets to shoot down the Vande Bharat flight.

As CO ATP 129 politely explained the ramifications of such an act, Boot In asked him to convey to the pip-squeak Indian NSA that both the truth about Game Zero and 'Ice Lilies' should be buried six feet under the earth the moment the aircraft landed in India lest he wanted to incur the Russian wrath. As Boot In cut the call and went back to sleep, CO ATP 129 booked a call for KB, and five minutes later, he was connected to him.

As Husn and Aashiq emerged from the staff entrance at 22:00 hours, Waxin Li, who was waiting in the shadows away from the CCTV cameras, whistled low to attract their attention. They met, and he led them to his Changer CS seventy-five, a popular Chinese car, parked nearby. Motioning them to get inside, he drove them to one of the small jetties on the still-flooded Yangtze River.

Waxin, probably the sharpest brain in China, had planned their escape meticulously. He knew that the Chinese Internal Security Service had a strong network of eyes and ears across the country and had anticipated that all surface, water and air routes would be blocked for them. He also foresaw that a big net, combining physical search and electronic surveillance, would be cast around the city limits of Wuhan to trap them; therefore, he decided to go underwater to escape.

The first thing he asked them to do as they got into the car was to change their attire, and as they were changing, he briefed them about their escape. The plan was to use DeepFlight Super Falcon thirty-five mini submarines to get out of the city limits of Wuhan. At a spot in the Hanan district, they would resurface and take a car to reach Lhasa by road via Xiaogan and Ankong; the route was longer, and the journey was more arduous but definitely much safer.

Husn's contacts from Lhasa would facilitate their movement to India. As Waxin was explaining the escape plan, Husn was texting it to Vidya, who had dozed off after the hearty meal.

As part of the plan, Waxin told Husn and Aashiq to place their mobiles under the car's tyres as they got out, and he drove over them, crushing them completely. His own mobile, he informed them, he had put around the neck of a Yak which was grazing near WVI. He was now carrying a use-and-throw untraceable SIM, which he had put in an old mobile phone that would be switched on only when required.

Luckily for Husn and Aashiq, just as Vidya dozed off, the matronly air hostess, a South Indian herself, asked if he would like a cup of filter coffee. On hearing filter coffee, Vidya was fully awake and nodded vigorously. He also read Husn's brain text and shook Sonny awake. Both of them agreed that while the escape plan was feasible and they could initially evade the Chinese Internal Security Service, but they would remain highly vulnerable during the two-day road journey to Lhasa. Vidya then decided to call his uncle once more.

AGAINST ALL ODDS

It was 04:00 hours in India, and Paddy was about to sit for his morning Puja. Slightly irked by the ring on his mobile, he noticed that Vidya was calling and decided to speak with him; in chaste Tamil, Vidya narrated to him the escape plan of Husn, Aashiq, and Waxin Li and their vulnerability during the road journey. As Paddy listened to Vidya, he realised that there was only one person in the country, known to Paddy, who was capable of snatching out Husn, Aashiq, and Waxin Li from the jaws of the Chinese dragon: General Aafat, the current Chief of Defence Staff!

Telling Vidya to call back in half an hour, he dialled Aafat's number. Unlike Paddy, Aafat was still in bed as he took the call. On hearing Paddy's anglicised tone, a smile crossed Aafat's face: he had interacted with Paddy since his Colonel days and respected him for his sharp mind and straight talk. Giving a brief background, Paddy narrated the escape plan and asked Aafat if he could help. Aafat requested Paddy to add Vidya to the call, and as Vidya wished him, he asked Vidya the current location of Waxin, Husn, and Aashiq and the means of communication available with the trio. Vidya replied that the current location of the trio would be inside the mini submarines deep in the waters of the Yangtze River, and the means of communication available with them was Waxin's old mobile and the brain texting backed up by the block chain system between the four of them.

Aafat then took down Vidya's mobile number and told him that he would be contacted by an officer of the Indian Army shortly in case the rescue operation was to go ahead. Telling Paddy that he would call him back to confirm either way, Aafat hung up and lay in his bed as he thought the issue through.

'The trio escaping from Wuhan was carrying the vaccine with them, which the whole world was desperately looking for to overcome the Coronavirus pandemic. If the vaccine came into the hands of Indian vaccine manufacturing companies, they would be able to mass produce enough doses for the country and the world. Otherwise, the pharma majors would make billions of dollars while a large segment of the Indian population would not be able to afford it. On the flip side, the armies of India and China were in an eyeball-to-eyeball confrontation for the last five months, and a slip-up in the rescue of the trio may start a shooting war that would be difficult to control.'

Gen Aafat was a hardened realist. He knew that India, like any other sensible country, could ill afford a war. In addition to avoidable loss of lives, it would push back the Indian economy by a decade. A vaccine against Coronavirus would be available in the next six to eight months, and the government of India would ensure inoculation of all its citizens in due course. But the soldier in him was not convinced. Successfully rescuing the trio would be a major advantage, as it would put the Chinese on the defensive. This would make them more open to negotiating a withdrawal of their forces, especially considering the sensitive information for the Indian side.

Suddenly, Aafat sprang out of his bed. His bold and audacious self this time helped him come to a conclusion. He knew that the moment the submarines carrying the trio surfaced, they would be vulnerable to the prying electronic and thermal imaging surveillance as well as the Chinese search parties. It would be a matter of time before the Chinese got their prey, so he had to act fast. He called up Mano Na Mano, who was already through with his early morning yoga and took the call in his office. After General Aafat had explained the whole issue to him, Mano Na Mano asked him only one question: what if the rescue mission failed? General Aafat replied that the Chinese would be very angry and aggressive, but the truth about Game Zero and the virus would help to cool their temper. Mano Na Mano gave his go-ahead.

Aafat gave a thumbs up to Paddy and Vidya, and then made two calls: first to Colonel Jang Bahadur Dubey, with the Director General Military Operations listening in. Jang Bahadur had recently been posted in Army HQ after commanding a Vikas Battalion for more than two years. A maverick, Jang Bahadur had served with the Special Forces, Rashtriya Rifles, Assam Rifles, National Security Guard and the Special Frontier Force. A free-faller and deep-sea diver, his uniform was aglitter with medals, badges and ribbons. Fearless, honest, committed, and physically fit, he was peerless but was a thorn in the backside if not handled well because of his penchant for calling a spade a shovel.

After being overlooked for promotion twice, he was all set to put in his papers when, much to his surprise, he got his promotion orders. Aafat first met him after Jang Bahadur successfully led the first Army expedition to Mount Everest without oxygen. Since then, he had remembered him as a daredevil.

As Aafat was connected to Jang Bahadur with the DGMO listening in, he instructed Jang to rush to Hashimara, an air force base in West Bengal, strategically located near the Chumbi Valley tri-junction of India, Bhutan, and China. His mission was to take a helicopter from Hashimara, fly into China, and retrieve the three individuals attempting to escape, with the Chinese in hot pursuit. Aafat assured Jang Bahadur that all necessary details would be provided during his flight to Hashimara, and then he ended the call. His second call was to Air Commodore Pashupatinath Prakash, Air Officer Commanding the Hashimara air base, with the Director of General Air Operations listening in.

Colonel Jang Bahadur, staying at Arjan Vihar, Delhi Cantonment, was fifteen minutes from the Palam air base, contiguous to the Indira Gandhi International Airport. Within ten minutes, he was in his car driving to the air base and picked up his battle gear and communication equipment from the National Security Guard HQ located just short of the airport.

As he entered the air base and parked his car near the briefing room, he could make out the silhouette of the small aircraft in the apron area. He picked up his battle gear and communication equipment, confirmed that the aircraft was for him, and boarded it. It had been twenty-seven minutes since General Aafat's call when Colonel Jang Bahadur boarded the aircraft. Three minutes later, the plane taxied to the runway and took off toward Hashimara. Two hours later, Colonel Jang Bahadur would be shaking hands with the AOC of Hashimara for the first time.

Though India has only one time zone, in actuality Hashimara is almost an hour ahead and while it was still dark in Delhi, Hashimara was already abuzz with early morning activity. Air Commodore Pashupatinath Prakash was was sweating it out on the treadmill when he was informed of the urgent call from the CDS.

Air Commodore Pashupatinath had met General Aafat for the first time as a young officer when he had been awarded the Vir Chakra for his daring helicopter-borne operations in Operation Pawan and then a year ago in Shillong, when General Aafat was being briefed by the Air Officer Commanding-in-Chief, Eastern Air Command. Air Commodore Pashupatinath hadn't noticed even a hint of recognition in General Aafat's eyes as he shook his hand and moved on, but unknown to him, General Aafat had an elephantine memory.

As he booked a call for AOC Hashimara, he recollected all professional and personal details of Air Commodore Pashupatinath: he knew that Pashupatinath, nicknamed PPT, was a gifted and daring helicopter pilot with a high sense of camaraderie and professional integrity. General Aafat also recollected that Pashupati's career was set back by a brain stroke, a heart attack, and suspected cancer, but true to his spirit, he had bounced back. For General Aafat, he was the man who could fly into China and rescue the trio against all odds.

As the operator put Air Commodore Pashupatinath and Director General Air Operations through, General Aafat, in a low monotone, explained the broad rescue plan and sought PPT's view. The DGAO was stunned by the audacity of the plan and its potential ramifications. Meanwhile, PPT informed Aafat that he would be flying a Chinook helicopter for the rescue mission. He sought for permission on two accounts: first, to land at Tawang for refueling both ways, and second, for full operational independence. As General Aafat agreed to both the requests, DGAO inquired if the Chief of Air Staff had been informed. Aafat told him that he would be speaking to both COAS and CAS and added that the rescue operation was TOP SECRET and nobody should know of it other than the two chiefs, DGMO & DGAO and of course Pashupatinath and Jang Bahadur.

After launching the escape plan, General Aafat named it Operation Tungba and briefed the Army and Air Force Chiefs on the details. While both were experienced combat professionals, they became concerned as the plan unfolded. They raised their concerns: Op Tungba relied on just two officers and one helicopter, with no backup plan in place. They pointed out that the Americans had sent over thirty SEALs in two helicopters to capture Osama Bin Laden, while China's surveillance and early warning systems were far more advanced than Pakistan's.

Aafat explained that more the number of helicopters and troops, bigger the electronic and physical footprint. Operation Tungba was an evade, rescue, and escape operation unlike Op Geronimo, which was a capture or kill operation ; moreover, Operation Tungba was time-critical. Without waiting for their replies, General Aafat hung up and went out for his early morning run. He would call KB two hours later as the Chinook carrying Colonel Jang Bahadur crossed the Line of Actual Control and entered Chinese territory.

Colonel Jang Bahadur spent the first forty-five minutes of his journey to Hashimara meditating, and then he called up Vidya on the mobile number given by General Aafat. He was told that the trio had successfully surfaced in Hannan district, boarded a car arranged by Waxin Li, and were on their way to Lhasa. After Vidya assured him that brain texting was completely secure, Colonel Jang Bahadur instructed him to inform the trio that the rescue operation was in progress. They were to find a hiding spot as soon as possible and stay there quietly through the day, as they would be more susceptible to detection while on the move. He also emphasized that the coordinates of their hiding place should be sent to him immediately, and all further communication should be done via brain texting only.

Vidya immediately brain texted the instructions to Husn, and she conveyed them verbatim to Waxin Li. In the next ten minutes, they got off the highway and onto a dirt track, which led them to a thick jungle. Waxin Li drove the car through the undergrowth, parked it under a natural canopy of trees, and killed the engine.

Dan spotted the mini-submarines floating idly on the Yangtze River in video footage of one of the UAVs searching for the trio. He knew that these submarines were a great tourist attraction but decided to have them checked as Coronavirus had killed tourism. An hour later, on receiving the report that the trio had apparently utilised the mini-submarines to escape, Dan and Kun Kar, who were also in the ad hoc Search Control Centre, moved immediately to have a closer look at the mini-submarines.

Colonel Jang Bahadur landed at Hashimara, was received by Air Commodore Pashupatinath on the tarmac itself, and taken to the Chinook helicopter parked in the apron area. There, as he munched on cucumber sandwiches, he was briefed about the mission by Air Commodore Pashupatinath. They were to head to Tawang, refuel, and enter into China through Tibet.

Pashupatinath spread out a map of China as Jang Bahadur gave him the coordinates of the trio's hiding place. He plotted the coordinates, marked the location, and calculated its distance. Pashupatinath realized that the distance from Tawang to the hideout exceeded the turnaround range of his Chinook. He found a densely wooded area near Chongqing with a small clearing large enough for the Chinook to land. After double-checking the distance from Tawang, he instructed Jang Bahadur that the trio should move to this location immediately. The chosen spot was a kilometre off the main road, tucked in the woods.

Col. Jang Bahadur got through to Vidya on mobile, who immediately brain texted the message to Husn. Within five minutes, the trio moved out of their hideout and were on their way to Chongqing.

Dan and Kun Kar reached the abandoned submarines and pieced together the underwater escape. Further inquiries helped them identify the car the trio had moved out in and the road they had taken. The chase was truly on now, with Kun Kar and Dan together in a car following the trail of the trio with a UAV focused on spotting the car; it was a matter of time before they got their prey. Unknown to them, the Li sisters, who had been briefed about the chase by number two, were following Kun Kar and Dan.

En route to Chongqing, Waxin Li stopped to refuel at a gas station and the car was spotted by the UAV; Kun Kar and Dan were but forty-five minutes away. Moments later, the electronic surveillance unit reported that Waxin Li's mobile had been traced and it was moving towards Urumqi, the capital of Xinjiang province; Waxin Li's sharp mind had played its last card.

Waxin knew that the abandoned submarines would be picked up; one thing would lead to another, and the search parties would be snapping at their heels in a matter of hours. He also knew that he would be expected to move to Urumqi more than any other place, so at the gas station, he had casually dropped his old mobile in the boot of a car going to Urumqi after switching it on.

After reaching the gas station, Kun, Kar, and Dan were in a quandary. While Waxin's mobile was moving towards Urumqi, the car carrying the trio had moved towards Chongqing. They finally decided to pursue Waxin's mobile, convinced that the movement of the car carrying the trio towards Chongqing was a ruse. Dan reasoned that Waxin's mobile was switched on at the gas station because he knew that it was the car that would be chased and that his safety lay in Urumqi. Dan instructed the UAV to track the car moving towards Urumqi as he and Kun Kar sped behind it. Waxin had managed to shake off the hounds, for some time at least.

Anne had managed to slip in a speck-sized but very powerful listening device in the car being driven by Dan as she coyly asked him for directions to Chongqing. The Li sisters overheard Dan and Kun Kar debating and deciding to follow the trio's car towards Chongqing. They were surprised to learn about Waxin Li, and as they were about to follow Dan and Kun Kar, Anne turned the car towards Chongqing. She reasoned that Dan and his men would definitely catch the trio if they moved to Urumqi. The Li sisters would catch them if they were moving towards Chongqing.

Pashupatinath took off from Hashimara, landed in Tawang in thirty minutes, refuelled and flew across the Line of Actual Control. Fifteen minutes later, General Aafat called KB on a secure line to inform him of Operation Tongba.

KB had gone through a round of gut-wrenching negotiations with CO ATP 129. Also, Mano Na Mano was quite tense when KB informed him that the Russians were all brimstone and fire on the escape of the Gang of Four, especially 'Ice Lilies', and demanded the immediate burial of the truth about Game Zero and the 'Ice Lilies'.

Although Mano Na Mano had said he was satisfied with KB's negotiations with the Russians, especially after their first demand was agreed to but the second one left vague, KB could sense the tension in his voice.

KB, though quite a daring guy himself, was taken aback at the audacity of Operation Tongba. He told General Aafat that Operation Tongba was hurriedly planned and had a high probability of failure. General Aafat was upfront and said that time was of the essence and any delay would have imposed an unacceptable time penalty.

KB reminded him of the explosive situation on the Line of Actual Control with China and how China would tighten the negotiating screws if they shot down the Chinook in their territory. General Aafat countered that the benefits in the form of the vaccine and the confirmation of WVI's involvement in developing and spreading the virus were well worth the risk of flying in the Chinook, and he was confident that Operation Tongba would succeed.

KB in a huff told General Aafat to inform Mano Na Mano about Operation Tongba personally. General Aafat permitted himself a smile as he confirmed in Garhwali, a local dialect of the Indian state of Uttarakhand, that he had already done so: both KB and General Aafat were from Uttarakhand and sometimes spoke in Garhwali.

The terrain across the Line of Actual Control was a seemingly endless landscape of brown and bald hilly outcrops rising out of flat high-altitude plains. Pashupatinath was utilising the valleys formed by the hilly outcrops for nap-of-the-earth flying to avoid detection. He was fortunate that Tibet is one of the most sparsely populated regions of the world, and there was no human settlement on his route to the pickup point. In addition, his Chinook had the same stealth technology as that of the Sikorsky UH-60 Black Hawk helicopter used in Operation Geronimo by the Americans to hunt down Osama Bin Laden.

Colonel Jang Bahadur's heart was in his mouth as Air Commodore Pashupatinath flew the Chinook at the treetop level, skillfully manoeuvring it to avoid obstacles like electric pylons, cables, and abrupt rocky jut-outs in the narrow valleys and defiles. Pashupatinath chuckled at Jang Bahadur's reaction and told him that it was better than being picked up by Chinese radars because he was not keen on undergoing Chinese torture!

They were about an hour and a half away from the pickup point.

The Vande Bharat flight carrying Vidya, Sonny, and the 'Ice Lilies' was thirty minutes from New Delhi when Captain Rai called KB. He had arranged for the Gang of Four to be picked up from the tarmac in an unmarked Intelligence Bureau (IB) car and taken to an IB safe house on Akbar Road. KB left for the safe house forty-five minutes later to personally debrief them.

As the Vande Bharat flight touched down at the Indira Gandhi International Airport, Vidya texted their arrival to Husn, but it was Aashiq who replied, saying they were half an hour away from the pickup point. Vidya texted it to Colonel Jung Bahadur, and he shouted it across to Air Commodore Pashupatinath.

Unknown to all of them, Li sisters, driving fast and hard, had closed up with the trio, and were about fifteen minutes behind as Waxin got off the highway near Chongqing and drove into a jungle lane; two kilometres and five minutes later they had hit the pickup point and Husn brain texted it to Vidya.

Colonel Jang Bahadur received the input a couple of minutes later and passed it on to Air Commodore Pashupatinath.

Five minutes later, Vidya received a message from Pashupatinath for the trio, 'the helicopter will be at the pickup point in thirty minutes, and they should be ready to climb onto it in a low hover'. He brain texted it to Husn.

Debriefing of the 'Gang of Four' commenced around the same time Vidya brain texted Pashupatinath's message to Husn, and it continued for two hours or so. Once KB was done with his penetrating questions, he told them that the Russians were wanting 'Ice Lilies' heads, and the best he could do for them was to help them lose themselves amongst approximately 1.4 billion Indians. They were off after a quick thank you to KB.

Li sisters took the same turn off the highway towards the pickup point but halted after driving for about two hundred metres. Their map showed a dead end after two kilometres of the jungle lane. They knew that their prey was close by, and they didn't want to give themselves away. Parking their car, the Li sisters broke into a run, keeping to either side of the road.

Ten minutes later, they spotted the car and tiptoed to the nearest tree to observe the area. They spotted the trio huddled together on the fringe of a clearing. Using sign language to communicate, they started closing in on their prey.

Air Commodore Pashupatinath's Chinook was five minutes away.

Getting closer to their prey soundlessly was proving to be doubly challenging for the Li sisters because of the fallen dried oak leaves. Four minutes had elapsed since they started closing in, and they were still fifty metres away from the trio. Anne realised that the crackling of the leaves might give them away, and she signalled to Mary to take out Aashiq with the poisonous dart as she aimed for Husn's slender neck; at fifty metres, the Li sisters were better with darts than pistols, and their targets were Husn and Aashiq. Waxin would be dealt with later.

The release of the two arrows, the appearance of the helicopter overhead and trio's movement towards it was near simultaneous. Waxin dropped dead as Anne's arrow hit the wrong neck, and Mary's arrow whistled past Aashiq's ear. Col Jang Bahadur helped Husn clamber up into the chopper, and as he reached out for Aashiq's hand, a bullet hit Aashiq's backside, and he collapsed on the ground; Li sisters had started shooting, and the helicopter, too, took a few hits.

In a flash, Colonel Jang Bahadur jumped off the helicopter, bodily picked up Aashiq, dumped him in the chopper, and hauled himself in as Air Commodore Pashupatinath pulled up the joystick to make a quick getaway. As the chopper gained height and swung away, Aashiq was in blinding pain, Husn was in a daze, and PPT turned a deaf ear to Col Jang Bahadur's entreaties to return and take out the Li sisters.

On the ground, the Li sisters checked on Waxin's inert body, confabulated for a couple of minutes, and then Anne called up the second-in-command in Shanghai; she gave him the lowdown on the duo's escape and Waxin's killing.

The second-in-Command asked her to wait there and called up Dan, who was about to take out the car that they were chasing through an armed UAV.

Blood drained off Dan's face as the second-in-command narrated the aerial escape of the duo. His initial reaction was a mixture of frustration, anger, and fear: fear of Winnie the Pooh's wrath. Dan closed his eyes, took a few deep breaths to clear his mind, and then told the second-in-command to pass him the coordinates of the pickup point and instruct the Li sisters to remain on-site. Aborting the attack on the Urumqi-bound car, he asked for a helicopter from the Chongqing PLAAF base.

Kun Kar nodded as Dan explained his decision to personally verify the information before reporting to Winnie the Pooh and notifying the PLAAF about the helicopter carrying Husn and Aashiq. He wanted to avoid a 'blue on blue' incident, similar to the one in the Kashmir Valley, where the IAF mistakenly shot down its own helicopter following the Balakot airstrike.

An hour had elapsed since Air Commodore Pashupatinath's hurried exit from the pickup point when Dan and Kun Kar landed there. They had a look at Waxin Li's inert body as Li sisters briefed them about the whole incident.

Having grasped the whole situation, Dan called Winnie the Pooh, briefed him, and tried to give a positive spin to his narrative, saying that they had got Waxin Li and PLAAF would shoot down the helicopter in which Hum and Aashiq had escaped once Winnie the Pooh gave his go-ahead.

Winnie the Pooh realised that Dan and his team had goofed up big time. Cold fury overtook Winnie the Pooh. He wanted to feed Dan to the crocodiles of Zhongnanhai lake but controlled himself and told Dan that PLAAF should locate and destroy the helicopter before it crossed into India and that he (Dan), should return to Beijing.

Kun Kar, the cunning old fox, had cleverly let Dan do the reporting to Winnie the Pooh and kept himself away from the botched-up operation; his survival instincts were legendary. To his dismay, however, Winnie the Pooh's next call was to him, and he was told to arrange for Waxin Li's body to be flown to Wuhan and a state funeral to be organised. Kun Kar sensed the tightness in Winnie the Pooh's voice but couldn't stop himself from asking why the state funeral.

Though tense, Winnie the Pooh replied that any adversity should be converted into an opportunity; the 'Economist' Magazine had recently published a damning article on the Chinese maltreatment of Uighur Muslims. Similarly, the American NSA had commented that the Chinese were committing genocide of Uighur Muslims, and the EU, too, was raising difficult questions of forced labour. A state funeral for a brilliant Uighur scientist who died of a heart attack while researching the vaccine for Coronavirus would convey to the world our feelings for the Uighurs. Ignoring the snigger from Kun Kar, Winnie the Pooh added that he would attend Waxin Li's funeral and announce a national award for him; it would further help dispel the misinformation campaign of the western World. Kun Kar was quick to praise Winnie the Pooh to high heavens for his brilliant stratagem before the latter hung up. Though Winnie the Pooh didn't acknowledge it, the praise made him feel good as he asked to be connected to Mano Na Mano. He hadn't shared the whole stratagem with Kun Kar.

One hour's lead time and the flying skills of Air Commodore Pashupatinath substantially increased the probability of evasion and escape from the PLAAF. Air Commodore Pashupatinath had chosen a different route but was stuck to nap-of-the-earth flying in the narrow valleys as the PLAAF launched a massive locate and destroy operation.

General Aafat was informed of the successful pick up of Husn and Aashiq and the Chinook's return journey to Tawang. General Aafat ordered five Rafael fighter aircrafts and an AWACS aircraft into the air, the latter to track the return of the Chinook and the former to deter Chinese aircraft from any misadventure.

After the aircraft was airborne, he updated Mano Na Mano on Operation Tongba.

Winnie the Pooh's call to Mano Na Mano materialised after General Aafat's update to Mano Na Mano. Winnie the Pooh blamed Mano Na Mano for violating China's sovereignty and threatened him with war. Mano Na

Mano feigned ignorance. The conversation, both tense and terse, went on for about twenty minutes. Finally, it was agreed that the Chinook inside Chinese territory was fair game but would not be shot down if it crossed the Line of Actual Control. Husn and Aashiq, if they lived, would not tell the tale, and the stolen formula of the vaccine would be shared with China. Both the leaders also agreed to keep the whole affair, including Operation Tongba, under wraps; total memory fade is what Winnie the Pooh had said.

After the call, Mano Na Mano thought that he had conceded a bit too much while Winnie the Pooh patted himself for retrieving a very ugly situation for his country. But he was still smarting at the audacity of the Indians and was keen to put them in their place by tightening the screws in Eastern Ladakh or elsewhere.

Air Commodore Pashupatinath's Chinook was fifteen minutes away from the Line of Actual Control when it was picked up by a Chinese satellite. Five minutes later, a Chinese aircraft readied itself to fire air-to-air missiles at the Chinook.

Luckily for Air Commodore Pashupatinath and others, the Indian AWACS aircraft picked up the movement of Chinese fighter aircraft and radioed Chinook to immediately gain height and release flares to confuse the heat-seeking missiles. Fortunately, Air Commodore Pashupatinath reflexively obeyed the command of the AWACS aircraft, gained height, and released the flares just before the missiles were released. Sure enough, both missiles, though fired at the Chinook, homed in on the more heat-generating target and missed the Chinook by a mile. The Chinese fighter aircraft sought permission to fire another pair of missiles, but it was denied as the Chinook was just about to cross the Line of Actual Control into the Indian side; the Chinese were also aware of the airborne Indian fighter aircrafts and had decided not to aggravate matters.

Seventeen minutes later, the Chinook landed at Tawang. There was another helicopter from the Aviation Research Centre also parked at the helipad. Husn handed over the vaccine sample and the formula to the Defence Research & Development Organisation Scientist, who had come from a laboratory in Gwalior, central India. The scientist uttered just a word of thanks and hurried over to board the ARC helicopter; he had to reach Bagdogra airport and take a special flight to Gwalior.

Husn and Aashiq got into a Tata Safari SUV, which took them to the Tawang Monastery, just six kilometres away. There they were received with open arms by the Buddhist monks of the monastery.

The Chinook, after refuelling, flew down to Hashimara and landed there in forty-five minutes. PPT dropped Colonel Jang Bahadur at the guesthouse and drove off to his residence. He went in for a bath as his wife readied for dinner. Colonel Jang Bahadur was informed that he was booked on a commercial flight to Delhi the next day. He put on his running shoes and went for a long run through the lush green tea gardens.

Epilogue

Immediately after the debrief, Vidya and 'Ice Lilies' got into a second-hand Toyota Innova, a popular car in India. They also had one Lakh rupee in their wallets; both the car and the money were loaned to them by KB. The car took Akbar Road and Sardar Patel Marg to move towards Gurugram. Vidya had planned to drive the 'Ice Lilies' to Goa and, after dropping them, drive off to Chennai. Ice Lilies were very excited about the prospect of being in Goa; they had heard a lot about its sun-kissed beaches, laid-back locals, and a large number of resident Russians.

Short of Manesar, Vidya decided to change Ice Lilies' destination to Rishikesh. Goa, he realised, also had a fearsome Russian mafia, and the FSB would most likely be overseeing it through a network of informers. He feared the thought of 'Ice Lilies' falling into the evil hands of the FSB. He informed 'Ice Lilies' of the change; they pouted in protest, and he turned onto the Eastern Periphery Expressway. The drive to Rishikesh took about five hours, with a break at the Cheetal Grand, an upscale roadside eatery.

Mano-Na-Mano continues to play his cards close to the chest even as General Aafat has termed the situation in Eastern Ladakh as tense, adding that the PLA was facing 'unanticipated consequences' for its misadventure in Eastern Ladakh.

KB and General Aafat are again on the best of terms after the success of Operation Tongba.

Bao Ching landed safely at the Hong Kong International Airport, also known as Chek Lap Kok Airport, along with his family and moved into an apartment in Mong Kok, the busiest commercial and residential district of Hong Kong; he thought that they would be safe in its maze of narrow lanes. Three weeks later, the apartment caught fire, apparently due to an electric short circuit, and the whole family died, their bodies totally charred. No post-mortem was carried out; otherwise, the cause of death would have been confirmed as poisoning, injected through deadly darts.

Lee sisters, as a reward, were flown to Shanghai where they were felicitated by the boss of the Big Circle Gang. They were offered permanent residency in Shanghai but preferred to return to the orderliness of Singapore.

Dan was purged by Winnie the Pooh, but Kun Kar played it smart and continues to be a member of the powerful communist committee and a close confidant of Winnie the Pooh. He has sworn revenge and activated his Tibetan agents to trace out Husn.

Winnie the Pooh has consolidated his hold over his party and the country and has got himself declared Supreme Leader.